The Green Gables Letters

About the Author

Wilfrid Eggleston (1901 - 1986) was born in England of parents who became pioneers in southern Alberta. After teaching in the West, he graduated from Queen's University, toured England, then began a newspaper career in Canada, on the staff of the *Toronto Star* and *Star Weekly*, in the parliamentary Press Gallery of the House of Commons in Ottawa, as well as political correspondent for *Reuters*, the *Manchester Guardian*, the *Financial Times* of Montreal, and the *Financial Post* of Toronto.

In 1937 he was a member of the secretariat of the Royal Commission of Dominion-Provincial Relations.

During World War II he was Director of Censorship for which he was awarded the M.B.E.

He held important posts with the Canadian Writers' Foundation, the Canada Foundation, and the International Press Institute; and Head of the Department of Journalism, Carleton University, Ottawa, where the **Wilfrid Eggleston Room**, was opened in the school of Journalism and Communications, 26 June 1997.

His published books include:

Prairie Moonlight and Other Lyrics (1927).
*The High Plains (a novel), (1938).
The Road to Nationhood (joint author, 1946).
Scientists at War (joint author, 1950).
Canada at Work (joint author, 1953).
The Frontier and Canadian Letters (1957).
*Prairie Symphony (a novel, 1978).
*Literary Friends (criticism, 1980).
*Homestead on the Range (autobiography, 1982).

*Available from Borealis Press

Preface to Second Edition

L.M. Montgomery was an indefatigable letter writer from an early age. When she was fifteen she left her beloved Island for the first time in her life with the intention of making her future home with her father and step-mother at Prince Albert, N.W.T. She did not find the new household congenial and soon became lonely for her old pals, but she found some consolation in furious exchanges of letters with friends and relations on the Island. Sixteen of her letters of that period, written to her cousin Penzie, were preserved and were thought by editors later on to be worthy of publication. The industry of Maud and her Island correspondents can be gleaned from the volume of their exchanges: she mentions having received three letters from P.E.I. by the same Prince Albert post; then five letters; and, on one glorious occasion, no fewer than eight letters had arrived by the same mail. All, of course, had to be answered without delay. By the time she was sixteen she was already a fluent and confident writer. Though some of the Prince Albert letters are no more than typical schoolgirl effusions, the best of her schoolday writing, in letters and in verse and in articles written for publication, is still interesting today and stands out for verve and literary flourish well above the millrun of similar juvenilia.

By the time she was in her twenties she had become a letter writer of such distinction that no apology is necessary on the part of any editor who proposes to include them within the permanent covers of a book. Some of the passages in them deserve a place in any anthology of Canadian literature. She had many correspondents in those early days: two of them were perceptive enough to realize that they had been so lucky as to find a kindred spirit who was "one in a million" among pen pals, and that her letters should be treasured and preserved like family heirlooms. In particular, the letters she wrote to Ephraim Weber and to George Boyd Macmillan add up to a substantial item in the bibliography of L.M. Montgomery. There is ample evidence, too, that she treasured their letters to her, that she found stimulation, inspiration and consolation in their friendship. As one token of her gratitude, she dedicated *Emily of New Moon* to George Boyd Macmillan in 1925, and *The Blue Castle* to Ephraim Weber in 1926. Even in the agony of her final days she could recognize and acknowledge what the exchanges of letters had meant throughout her adult life. "Let us thank God," she wrote in one of her final notes to Weber, "for a long and true friendship." To Macmillan, in her last letter, she wrote: "There are few things in my life I have prized as much as your friendship and letters."

The correspondence with Ephraim Weber began in 1902. A glance at the emotional and social *milieu* or ambience of her life at the time makes it clear why she hungered so desperately for mature, intimate, spiritual and literary contacts, such as she was able to find in a developing correspondence with two kindred spirits. She was currently an emotional "shut in"; she was imprisoned in a stifling moral atmosphere; such letters offered a delightful release. In one of her early letters to Macmillan she confessed that "the outward circumstances of my life are at present miserably circumscribed and carking." This was, she explained, "owing in great measure to poor old grandmother's age and rapidly increasing childishness." She didn't think, indeed, that she would have the courage or strength to endure her imprisonment if she could not escape from it "into a world of the fancy."

Exactly what she meant by "circumscribed and carking" in reference to her life at Cavendish can be documented in detail by her own testimony. It will already be familiar to all students of her works. It is sufficient here to recall the essential elements. It all stemmed from the sad fact that her beloved mother had died when she was less than two years old and that she had been brought up by her maternal grandparents: Alexander Maquis Macneill and Lucy Anne Woolner (Macneill). They had provided her with all the material necessities of life and she was grateful for that, but she felt in later years that they had been unwise and even unkind in their treatment of her in other ways. She resented the fact that they had shut her off as a small girl from "all social life, even such as this small country settlement could offer" and had debarred her "from the companionship of other children and—in early youth—other young people." They were upright, stern, strict, Victorian.

She escaped from this moral prison when she was fifteen. Her father had become a restless traveller after his first wife died and by 1890 he was well established in the North West Territories. He had taken a second wife and had set up a family and a household in Prince Albert. L.M. Montgomery at fifteen decided that she would like to go west and live with her father, and this was agreed upon. But once in the new home she found the relationship with her stepmother increasingly uncongenial and a year later she returned to her beloved Island. She was now old enough to prepare herself for entrance to Prince of Wales College at Charlottetown; and in the next five years she set out on an ambitious career as student, school teacher and freelance writer, at Halifax, Charlottetown and other Island centres. At that stage she seemed to have emerged forever from the "circumscribed and carking" environment of her girlhood.

Then, in March, 1898, when she was twenty-three and teaching school at Lower Bedeque, a sudden bereavement confronted her with a cruel dilemma. Her grandfather died suddenly, and the Cavendish home in which L.M. Montgomery had spent her first fifteen years was faced with extinction. Grandmother Woolner Macneill would have to go and live with other relatives and the Cavendish house and farm would be taken over by Uncle John. Grandfather had been the Cavendish postmaster since 1870; and her Grandmother would have been a logical successor, but she could not take it on without help.

Maud Montgomery came to the rescue. She offered to terminate her teaching contract at Lower Bedeque at once and come to live again with her grandmother at Cavendish. She could be appointed assistant postmistress at Cavendish, and between them she and her grandmother could manage quite well, financially and otherwise. By this time L.M. Montgomery had won sufficient ground in her freelance activities to virtually ensure that she could make as good an income from freelance writing at Cavendish as she had from school teaching in country schools on the Island.

It was a generous gesture and for a while Maud Montgomery seems to have been reconciled to the cost in personal freedom and in the submission to "circumscribed and carking conditions." But as her grandmother grew older and "more childish" the sacrifice grew heavier. By the time her correspondence began with Ephraim Weber in 1902 she was ready to pounce on any opportunity to break out of her narrow social boundaries. She relied more and more on her diaries, her poetry, her essays and short stories, and her correspondence with "kindred spirits."

Montgomery's long-distance friendship with Weber and Macmillan began in a most improbable way. There was nothing planned or designed about it; L.M. Montgomery did not initiate the original contacts. Both Ephraim Weber and George Macmillan—complete strangers to her, and living five thousand miles apart—were virtually ordered, by a distant third party whom L.M. Montgomery hardly knew—to enter into correspondence with her. So in a sense the friendships were a sort of happy chance, or divine gift. These boons fell into her lap without any effort on her part, but she had the prescience to know a good thing when she encountered it.

About the turn of the century an industrious Philadelphia scribbler named Miriam Zieber began to build up a stable of pen-pals from the names of authors gleaned from the current magazines. She conceived the idea of organizing a sort of gloried "Mutual Aid Society" of struggling writers, an exclusive club whose membership would be chosen by herself. They would help one another climb to the top. Her ultimate dream was to establish in her own house in Philadelphia a coterie of the chosen few. They would pay board and room and help one another supply the magazines of North America and the British Isles with suitable literary fare. She had seen Ephraim Weber's name attached to some pleasant verse in one of the Sunday School magazines and began a correspondence. In one of their exchanges (presumably late in 1901) Weber happened to mention that he had been much impressed with some poetic lines signed "L.M. Montgomery" and he added that if he knew where "Mr. Montgomery" lived he'd write and tell him so. Miss Zieber wrote back jubilantly that L.M. Montgomery was already one of *her* "pen-pals"; that L.M. stood for Lucy Maud; and that Ephraim Weber must write to her and declare his admiration.

Weber bashfully demurred, but Miss Zieber was not to be denied. When Weber did write it was in a different tone; the idea was entirely Miss Zieber's; Miss Montgomery "need not write before convenient"; still, he hopes to hear from her.

In 1903 Miss Zieber decided that George Boyd Macmillan, a young printer living in Alloa, Scotland, would also be a suitable correspondent for L.M. Montgomery. Macmillan writes to her; and she replies that she will be very pleased to carry on a literary correspondence with him, especially so since he lives in Scotland, the home of so many of her ancestors.

Miss Zieber pursued her idea of assembling in Philadelphia a club of freelance writers; and her influence over Ephraim Weber was strong enough to induce him to borrow money on his homestead and move to Philadelphia in the fall of 1902. But he was no more successful as freelance writer in Philadelphia than he had been in Alberta; and a few months later he returned to his homestead north of Calgary, poorer but wiser, with his finances "fractured," as he wrote L.M. Montgomery. But Miss Zieber's invitations to L.M. Montgomery and George Macmillan to come to Philadelphia were in vain. They couldn't get away.

On the face of it, Ephraim Weber did not sound at first like a suitable "pen-pal" for L.M. Montgomery. Their backgrounds and early literary experiences were so far apart. Montgomery was already, in 1902, a going concern as freelance writer; she had been placing scripts in magazines and newspapers for twelve years; she had been raised in a home and in a community where literary values were cherished and respected. Weber, in great contrast, was the older son of a plodding Mennonite farmer of Waterloo County, Ontario, in a family which spoke only Pennsylvania Dutch, an unlettered family ("my parents have never heard of Shakespeare," he later wrote). He was twelve years old before he spoke his first sentence in English. His schooling in English began so late that he was still at high school when he entered his twenty-third year. But Ephraim Weber was not a typical Mennonite farm boy. Once he made up his mind to get an education, he set out on a course which culminated when he completed (at age 47) all the classwork for a degree of Doctor of Philosophy at the University of Chicago, having meanwhile picked up the degrees of Bachelor of Arts and Master of Arts, together with Medals in French and German, at Queen's University, Kingston. He had acquired along the way a passionate love of lyric poetry and an ambition to write great books. More important, so far as the friendship with L.M. Montgomery is concerned, he grew into an original thinker, a fascinating correspondent, a letter writer of style and flavour out of the ordinary. I write with some conviction on these points: he was my own teacher, mentor, spiritual confidant and true friend for over thirty-five years, until his death. So I had no difficulty comprehending the high value L.M. Montgomery placed on his friendship. (My mother told me that Mr. Weber was "the finest Canadian" she had ever met.) It is a happy accident of Canadian letters that so many of the letters between Ephraim Weber and L.M. Montgomery were saved. He inspired her to write a sequence of letters of outstanding charm, which are available in the present volume.

Ottawa, 1981   Wilfrid Eggleston

Acknowledgments

My personal debt to Ephraim Weber is so great that I was happy to do something for his memory in the course of preparing this collection. He was teacher, counsellor, guide and critic during a turning point in my own life. In the Lajord and Outlook days, Mrs. Weber was a second mother to a youth far from home. I am grateful to her for many things, not least for her great kindness in making these letters available to me and for supplying me with so much additional biographical material about her late husband. Dr. Stuart Macdonald, younger son and literary executor of L. M. Montgomery, added tremendously to the pleasure of editing these letters by uncovering for me the whole file of the Weber letters to his mother, and by giving me a free hand in their use. They added another dimension to the Cavendish letters as printed here; without them it would have been a bit like hearing one side only of a telephone conversation. To Mrs. H. D. McCorquodale of High River, Alberta, a contemporary of Mrs. Weber's in the Didsbury Public School teaching days, I owe some interesting notes and impressions of the period 1906-1909. My wife, Magdelana, not only provided practical help in typing the book but supplied an early enthusiasm and perception of the appeal of these letters which was a large factor in persuading me to prepare them for publication. Dr. Lorne Pierce, as he has done so often before, converted what might have remained a vague intention into a solid achievement.

W.E.

General Introduction

I

These wise and witty letters by the author of *Anne of Green Gables* were written at Cavendish, on the "old north shore" of Prince Edward Island, and addressed to a friend in far-away Alberta. The correspondence began in 1902, when a homesteader of literary tastes wrote a "fan letter" to a freelance just beginning to make her mark in the American magazines. Ephraim Weber was living in his pioneer shack or "den" about fifty miles north of Calgary when the exchange of letters opened. To his great and increasing delight he found a personality after his own heart in this industrious versifier and weaver of girls' stories; and the correspondence flourished. L. M. Montgomery, in turn, discovered in the Alberta homesteader a rare and original spirit of increasing fascination. It was a Platonic attachment on both sides, but so vital was the comradeship that the correspondence thus begun in 1902 ceased only with her last illness nearly forty years later.

The first L. M. Montgomery letter, printed below in full, carries the date March 7, 1905. Unhappily, many of her earliest letters to Ephraim Weber have been lost. He valued and cherished them from the very beginning, as his own letters to her, systematically filed away at Cavendish by L. M. Montgomery, clearly show. He keenly regretted in later years his carelessness and lack of foresight in not saving all of hers. "I have not kept many of your letters, for I innocently assumed I'd be getting new ones indefinitely," he told her at a later date. "When people are alive and moving they don't have to subsist on the past." He might have added in his own defence that between 1902 and 1905 he was living in bachelor's shacks and in tents, camping out on the fringes of settlement, and, in between, going on a tour to Philadelphia, New Hampshire and Ontario.

By good fortune, however, an important sequence of letters covering an influential and critical period in the rise of L. M. Montgomery as a famous author survived all hazards and later wanderings of Ephraim Weber back and forth across the North

1

American continent. They were found among his papers, after his death at Victoria, B.C., in March, 1956, most of them still in the original covers. The letters reproduced here exactly as they were written are now lodged in the National Archives at Ottawa.

The interest and importance of the letters written by L. M. Montgomery between 1905 and 1909 lies partly, of course, in the fact that these were the years of gestation and birth and outstanding success of the book *Anne of Green Gables*, which converted her almost overnight from a struggling contributor to a host of magazines, celebrated and obscure, into one of the literary sensations of the era.

In this sense they form a fascinating footnote to the history of Canadian letters, for entirely aside from the merits of *Anne of Green Gables* as a story for girls, its publication marks one of the most impressive success stories of Canadian authorship. But the printing of them requires no justification on this or on any other score. They can be read with pleasure for their literary flavour and for their revelations of a lively and attractive personality, even if the reader has not hitherto read a single line of the famous Anne books or their successors. As Mr. Weber wrote in an appraisal after her death, there was not a single careless or perfunctory line in all the forty years of her correspondence. I have read these Cavendish letters over and over again, and find that their charm persists and their freshness never fades.

II

During the late winter of 1902, Ephraim Weber was "baching it" in his homestead "den" situated about three miles east of the recently founded settlement of Didsbury, on the Calgary-Edmonton railway line. One day in March he sat down at his kitchen table to address a letter to a young lady in the Maritimes, a person quite unknown to him except as a name attached to some pleasant nature lyrics he had noticed in some recent magazines. Something of the etiquette of the times and of his own delicate sensibilities can be inferred from the fact that he did not even allow himself to address her, "Dear Miss Montgomery." Instead he merely wrote her name and address at the top of a single sheet of social notepaper and began abruptly as follows:

"Miss Zieber says I am to write to you. She tells me she has obtained permission for me to do so, and that she is sure a correspondence between us would give us both much pleasure and literary edification. The idea is altogether hers, and I hope she is right."

L. M. Montgomery treasured his letters to her as much as he did hers to him; and being of a more methodical inclination and in a more settled residence, she kept them all, fastened together by narrow ribbons inserted through the corner, neatly contained in a series of folders, each inscribed with the inclusive dates. Through the courtesy of Dr. Stuart Macdonald, younger son and literary executor of the novelist, I have this earliest communication and all the succeeding letters from Ephraim Weber before me as I write.

In the next paragraph he came to the point. He had seen three of her poems, and had liked them. He was trying to write poetry himself. To be specific, he had read "The Cure of the Fields" in the *Sunday School Times*. He had read "Harbour Dawn" in the *Family Herald* of Montreal, and "Harbour Sunset" in *Current Literature*. Moreover, Miss Zieber had informed him that she had had several poems in *Youth's Companion*. Would she let him know the dates of two or three numbers containing her work, so that he could send for them? "Let me congratulate you heartily upon so much success in a difficult art. Do you also write prose?" Then, referring to the fact she was currently employed on the staff of the Halifax *Echo*, he observed: "You must be very busy."

He confesses that he has very little to boast about in the writing line. "I am provokingly unproductive. It is only a year since I began trying to write with an object, although I have dabbled on and off at composition for ever so long a time. During the past five years I had occasional acceptances by a magazinelet of small pay. In 1901 I managed to get into honourable print with two pieces, a short essay and a quatrain, but I have not yet been able to do as much again."

He hopes to see more of her poetry soon, for he is practising the same art with a view to publication. He knows no Canadian writers at all. "We have nearly the whole continent between us, but that doesn't matter."

"I shall await your reply with pleasure, but you need not write before convenient," he concludes, signing himself "Yours fraternally, Ephraim Weber."

He was thirty-one when he wrote this letter; she was twenty-seven. The letter was addressed to Halifax. The *Daily Echo* was an evening edition of the Halifax *Chronicle*. L. M. Montgomery, as he learned later, was engaged in general reporting, ran a weekly social column called "Around the Tea Table" and performed the usual variety of jobs required in a small newspaper office.

III

Ephraim Weber's first letter was dated March 12th and L. M. Montgomery's reply March 29th. Allowing for the time needed to carry them across the continent this was a prompt response. Her early letters, as I have said, are no longer in existence, but an active correspondence grew up almost immediately, so that by late spring there was an almost continuous exchange. It is safe to assume from the tenor of his letters that she encouraged him to continue and found the prospect of his correspondence highly acceptable. Each discovered in the other an engaging and stimulating personality. The fact that the correspondence flourished, as I have said, for forty years, suggests that a deep bond of friendship was being woven in those early days. The letters grow longer and more confidential, more revealing. The friendship was Platonic, but its intensity developed. The single sheet of notepaper became two, three, four, eight and ten. Some of his earlier letters ran to sixteen and eighteen pages. Even after a quarter of a century their letters, by now Christmas "annuals" for the most part, ran up to bulky packages of five or six thousand words. When the correspondence began both of them enjoyed relative leisure and tranquillity, but when circumstances changed materially the flow continued. In 1908 L. M. Montgomery suddenly shot into prominence as the author of a best seller. From then on she had to handle a large miscellaneous correspondence and satisfy her increasingly importunate publishers. In 1911 she became the wife of a Presbyterian minister and in due course the mother of two lively boys. Her industry in church work, Red Cross work, amateur theatricals, recitals, addresses, was prodigious. Her "fan" mail alone at times demanded almost full-time attention. She was always a prolific correspondent, but as time wore on the pressure of other duties compelled her to drop one after another of her old epistolary connections. Only two endured to the end. One of these was George Boyd Macmillan of Alloa, Scotland, to whom she dedicated *Emily of New Moon*. The other, oldest and most favoured friend of all, was Ephraim Weber, to whom she dedicated *The Blue Castle*. Their exchange of letters was unique in the life of two outstanding practitioners of the epistolary art.

Yet this remarkable correspondence arose in a curiously casual way. Ephraim Weber, it is clear, was virtually coerced into beginning it. Who was this Miriam Zieber whose name occurs so frequently in the letters?

There was an air of coincidence and improbability about the whole matter. Miss Zieber was an aspiring scribbler of Philadelphia, much given to shop talk and literary pen pals. In some manner which doesn't appear in the correspondence she began exchanging letters with L. M. Montgomery of Cavendish, P.E.I., about the turn of the century. A little later she must have seen Ephraim Weber's name attached to some essay or fragment of verse in the *Sunday School Times*, and she added his name to her list of correspondents.

In one of his own early letters from the North West Territories to Miss Zieber at Philadelphia, Ephraim Weber mentioned in passing that he had seen and liked a poem signed L. M. Montgomery. He supposed that the said Montgomery was a man, and confided to Miss Zieber that if he knew where "Mr." Montgomery lived he'd send him a note of gratitude and appreciation. Miss Zieber triumphantly wrote back that Miss Montgomery was a young lady whose home was in Prince Edward Island, but who was temporarily on the staff of a newspaper in Halifax, having gone there for the winter. The rest of the incident is explained by the wording of Mr. Weber's first letter quoted above. Miss Zieber, who had a forceful if not indeed something of a domineering nature, insisted that he overcome his native bashfulness, and write to the Maritime poetess direct to declare his admiration.

So the correspondence began. As it developed, each of them began, both unconsciously and deliberately, to tell a bit more about themselves. Their personalities and backgrounds began to take on colour and detail. We do not know exactly what L. M. Montgomery wrote in the missing letters, but the story she had to tell was admirably sketched out in a brief autobiography she prepared some years later.

I was born—praise to the gods!—in Prince Edward Island, that colourful little land of ruby and emerald and sapphire (she wrote). I come of Scotch ancestry with a dash of English from several "grands" and "greats." My mother died when I was a baby and I was brought up by my grandparents in the old Macneill homestead at Cavendish, eleven miles from a railway and twenty-four from a town, but only half a mile from one of the finest sea-beaches in the world, the "old north shore."

I went to the district school from six to sixteen. Out of school I lived a simple, wholesome, happy life, on the old farm, ranging through fields and woods, climbing over the rocky "capes" at the shore, picking berries in the "barrens" and apples in the big orchards. I am especially thankful that my childhood was spent in a spot where there were many trees—trees with personalities of their own, planted and tended by hands long dead, bound up with everything of joy and sorrow that visited my life, a life that was very simple and quiet. But it never held a dull moment for me. I had, in my imagination, a passport to fairyland. In a twinkling I could whisk myself into regions of wonderful adventure, unhampered by any restrictions of reality.

I was a great reader and devoured every book I could lay hands on no matter what it was. Novels were taboo but fortunately there was no ban on poetry. I could revel at will in the "music of the immortals"—Longfellow, Tennyson, Whittier, Scott, Byron, Milton, Burns. And one wonderful day when I was nine years old I discovered I could write "poetry" myself.

It was called *Autumn* and I wrote it on the back of an old postoffice "letter bill"—for writing-paper was not too plentiful in that old farmhouse, where nothing was ever written save an occasional letter. Father said it didn't sound like poetry. "It's blank verse," I cried. "Very blank," said father.

I determined that my next poem should be rhymed. And I wrote yards of verses about flowers and months and trees and stars and sunsets and addressed "lines" to my friends. When I was thirteen I began sending my verses to the Island weekly papers—and never heard either of or from them. Perhaps this was because I did not send any return stamps, being in blissful ignorance of such a requirement.

Before this, however, when I was eleven years old, I had

begun writing stories. I had a boxful of them, very tragic creations in which almost everybody died. In those tales battle, murder and sudden death were the order of the day.

When I was fifteen I had my first ride on a railway train, and it was a long one. I went out to Prince Albert, Saskatchewan, and spent a year with father who was living there then. During that winter I sent a "poem" written around one of the dramatic legends of the old north shore of the Island, down to the Charlottetown *Patriot*. And the *Patriot* printed it, thereby giving me the greatest moment of my life.

Being now, as I thought, fairly launched on a career, I kept on sending verses to various papers and begun to plume myself on being quite a literary person. I returned to Prince Edward Island the next summer, attended school for another year, then went for a year to Prince of Wales College, Charlottetown, to qualify for a teacher's license. After that I taught a year. During these years I was writing all sorts of stuff, mainly verses and short stories, but had never succeeded in getting into any periodical that paid anything. All the stuff I sent to other magazines came promptly back. I used to feel woefully discouraged at times over those icy little rejection slips. But I kept on. Whatever gifts the gods had denied me they had at least dowered me with stick-to-it-iveness.

After teaching a year I went to Halifax and spent a winter taking a selected course in English literature at Dalhousie College. One day in that winter I got a letter from the editor of an American juvenile magazine, accepting a short story I had sent him and enclosing a cheque for five whole dollars. Never in all my life have I felt as rich as I did then.

I taught two more years. Then grandfather died, and I went home to stay with grandmother. She and I lived there together in the old farmhouse.

To bring the narrative right up to the minute, L. M. Montgomery could have added: "Last November [1901] I came here to work as proofreader and general handyman on the staff of the *Daily Echo*."

IV

From his early letters, L. M. Montgomery learned much about Ephraim Weber's views and current activities, but tantalizingly little about his background, origins, family circumstances or education.   In her first letter, unfortunately not extant, she inquired about his name and birthplace.   "Yes, I am Canadian born," he wrote back in reply.   "Are you?   My parents are, too, and my grandparents were born in Pennsylvania, as were my great-grandparents, as I once heard a specialist in the origin of Pennsylvania German families declare—for you perceive that my name is German.   At home amongst ourselves we speak this language but we are thoroughly Canadian."   Two months later he confides a bit about his religious upbringing. A literary society has sprung up at Didsbury, he relates, and he is secretary of it, and will be captain in a forthcoming debate. They meet in the Presbyterian Church, though he was brought up a Mennonite.   "So you see, I'm no respecter of persons either. I cannot now be said to have any particular creed, though I'm no infidel or iconoclast or anything of that dreadful sort, for I teach a large little class of young men and women in the Mennonite Sunday School, and so far as I know, my name is still on the church roll.   It was long the only church here, so I clung to it because I liked the people rather than the church.   Have you ever heard of the Mennonites?   There are several varieties, of course.   They don't differ as much from the Methodists, Baptists and U. Brethren as you may fancy."

In his next letter he tells her about his writing ambitions and his small successes to date.   "My thin, scattered, crestfallen contributions, in their *grand totality*, have brought me $75 more or less.   I began scribbling six years ago, but since then I've also taught in an excuse for private school, been knocking about on our homesteads, been assessor, poll-clerk, deputy returning officer at elections and census-taker for a huge area."

In August he confesses a literary passion.   "Last night I read an essay on Tennyson before the Literary Society.   I dwelt mainly on his 'verbal magic,' quoting from 'The Revenge,' 'The May Queen,' 'In the Children's Hospital' and 'Ulysses.'   But I might as well try to rope the rainbow as to try to analyze his magic.   Isn't poetry the human soul's magic come out to sun itself in the grace of language?"   His love of Tennyson, he hints, was chiefly engendered by the headmaster at the old Berlin High School, one J. W. Connor.   "I remember when Tennyson died," he goes on. "We were studying his poetry at school that year, and the old headmaster came in for the literature lesson one day with the tears rolling down his broad grey beard and choked with emotion. Without saying a word, he wrote 'Crossing the Bar' on the blackboard, and after a perfect silence of fifteen minutes, he read it aloud. I have never since heard poetry read so effectively. The lyric is altogether sacred to me." Several months later, he and L. M. Montgomery exchanged confidences about their first published poems. "I thought my heart would jump out of my mouth and dance a waltz down the path when my teacher surprised me by showing me a local paper containing my poem on 'The Bird and the Boy,' which I had handed to him as my weekly 'Composition' the previous Friday," he wrote, "I made the bereft birdie say—

> At evening the whip-poor-will lulls me to sleep,
> At morning the skylark awakes me to weep.

This is great pathos, though I was then well up in my teens."

There is not much more autobiography, in the 25,000 words or so of correspondence he wrote to L. M. Montgomery between 1902 and early 1905. He confesses that he has never learned to dance, since "I was brought up under the notion that the devil had a hand in this sort of thing." He envied her the bookish atmosphere of her earliest childhood. She had, as it were, been *born* into reading, whereas he had had to "grind and chisel" himself into it. "Our race are not at all for intellect and culture. My parents have never heard of Shakespeare." Long afterwards he added: "I was twelve before I spoke an English sentence. I didn't read anything until I was an adult. Such was my heredity and environment, and to this day I suffer from it."

V

Since Ephraim Weber may be regarded as the "onlie begetter" of this sheaf of letters by L. M. Montgomery, the reader is entitled to something more substantial in the way of a bio-graphical sketch than can be gleaned from his early letters to L. M. Montgomery. As he was one of my own dearest personal friends from 1918 until his death in 1956, this should not be too difficult to provide. He was almost abnormally reticent about his family background and upbringing, however, and it was not until he was in his seventy-fifth year that I was able to coax him into answering a number of questions on these topics. Since then I have been able to fill out some of the vaguer passages from material kindly supplied to me by his widow, Annie Campbell Melrose (Mrs. Ephraim Weber), of Victoria, B.C.

He was born on November 20, 1870, on his father's farm at Bridgeport, just outside the city limits of Berlin, Ontario. His home was a mile from the Grand River. He was the oldest of a family of four sons and a daughter born to Andrew Weber and Veronica Shantz. His first nineteen years were spent on the farm. It was a niggardly holding, I gather, and his father eked out a thin livelihood by part-time work as an agent. This took him away for long periods, during which the burden of farm work fell upon the oldest son. He never talked much about the early days, but there are a few interesting fragments in his correspondence. In one of the last letters he ever wrote, he remembered himself as a plow boy: "In my farming days I got so far as to go to a plowing match once—so far as the limits of Waterloo Township! Our farm facing on much-travelled Lancaster St., I had to plow straight furrows, to suit Dad, at least when they ran at right-angles to the street; and once I overheard Dad agreeing with a neighbour how straight my furrows were, which tickled my new pride." Mrs. Weber commented on this: "He plowed when too young, so that he became a bit round-shouldered."

When Mabel Dunham of Kitchener wrote a book about the Grand River, it evoked from him a few memories. Writing to Leslie Staebler, a "bosom companion" of his Berlin High School days, he said: "I know Mabel Dunham very scantily, except as the author of *The Trail of the Conestoga*. Now on a pension in retirement? And at work on another Waterloo County book, *The Valley of the Grand*? I grew up only a long mile from it, saw it a thousand times in all its moods and sizes and sylvan bends. For years there were two rivers on earth: the Grand and the Irrawaddy! I went to school at Bridgeport on the Grand, and the catchy name of the other stuck in my ear. I fancied this stream was wide, wide, and long, long, and perhaps even half again as big and deep as the Grand, but if I had known that the Grand was big and important enough to have a *book* written about it, I'd have easily classed it with the Irrawaddy, which was so far, far away, maybe seven hills and ten swamps away, among tigers."

When Mabel Dunham's book on the Grand River was published, and he had read it, it evoked another fragment of octogenarian nostalgia. "The old river we used to go a mile to bathe and splash in on a warm Saturday evening has assumed some little majesty for me; and I love to recall its huddly beauty of scenery at Bridgeport (our sheep used to be washed in it there) and the jungled banks where we used to swim, and the lovely plains with tall trees where it flowed past Natchez where my father grew up—under the big hill; a spot of bucolic beauty."

In a note he once made for me about his origins, Ephraim Weber wrote: "Go four or five generations back and you'll find us newly arrived from Pennsylvania, speaking the Pennsylvania Dutch dialect of German, several counties of it. I see by my brother's record we had some little of United Empire Loyalist in us. Our mother's father (Jacob Y. Shantz) was a grand old settler, alert, devoted, practical, pious. Our religion was the Mennonite faith, until recently; many of us widened out, in fact the religious leaders in various regions got surprisingly liberal, grandpa Shantz going so far as to join Christian Science."

On his father's side, Ephraim Weber's most illustrious forebear was his great-grandfather, Bishop Benjamin Eby, one of the leading Mennonite pioneers of Waterloo County. His mother's father, however, the "Grandpa Shantz" referred to above, cut a more prominent figure in Canadian history than any other family connection. Jacob Y. Shantz, as the leading building contractor of that thriving community, built the first Berlin town hall; and in 1872 he was commissioned by the government of Sir John A. Macdonald to manage a large immigration and settlement scheme, under which thousands of Mennonites fleeing from religious persecution in Europe were successfully placed in the new province of Manitoba. Again there is a tiny but vivid glimpse from Ephraim Weber's pen. Writing about Mabel Dunham's *Grand River* book, he commented: "So that's how the Grand River country came about? Most of it fresh and new to me. That bit about my Grandpa Shantz I might wish a trifle amplified, were it only the bit I remember him telling us boys about the buffalo stampede in Manitoba on one of his Mennonite-settling trips, when his Red-River-Carts party was held up the bigger part of an afternoon by migrating buffalo in a wide stream."

A later reference to Mabel Dunham elicited another fragment of reminiscence: "While I'm about it, let me tell how we Webers enjoyed reading her *Trail of the Conestoga*, which she has so deliciously spiced with our native Pennsylvania Dutch in getting those Woolichers settled. How we laughed to hear our precious childhood idioms again, after so many years' neglect of them, as we took turns in reading it out to one another in the presence of Elsie's husband and my wife, who wondered what the laughing was all about, and whose laughs were merely an echo of our own.   Even our sickly mother laughed in sympathy—her dear last little laughs ever."

By the time he was nineteen, Ephraim Weber had become a highly discontented and frustrated Mennonite farm hand, and no wonder.   He rebelled at the limitations of his environment. In his own words, he "took a notion to have an education, and returned to public school."   He thought he might become a school teacher.   It could not have been less than an ordeal to go back to grade school and sit with children six or eight years younger.   But he made good.   Indeed, he passed the entrance examinations with the highest mark in Waterloo County.   This qualified him to enroll in Berlin High School, where he revelled in literature, grammar and composition.   He always spoke highly of the headmaster, J. W. Connor, and two or three of Connor's teaching associates.   And he made several lifelong friends among the classmates.   It is an interesting sidelight that one of his friends and fellow pupils was the son of a Berlin lawyer, "Rex" or "Billy" King as the boys knew him.   "I remember the lovely woodsy home he was brought up in," Mr. Weber wrote me, "and can still see Billy driving his father in a two-seated gig to his law office, before going to high school in the mornings." Hon. W. D. Euler was another classmate.   Mr. Weber thought that the future prime minister of Canada, like himself, had caught something of enduring virtue from J. W. Connor.   He went into this in a letter written to L. M. Montgomery in 1912; and after Mackenzie King's death he wrote Leslie Staebler, his most cherished schoolmate, as follows: "So there's no William Lyon Mackenzie King in the flesh now?   Well, he set a personality going on earth that, I believe, tallies upliftingly in its great way— not that all his ways were great.   His conciliatory talent and his culture always appealed to me.   In his cultured English I always heard and smacked the literary refinement of our great Jimmy Connor."   Weber remembered King as "our star debater" at Berlin High School; who, however, sometimes lost his debates. Writing to me at about the same time (August, 1950), Ephraim Weber added some remarks that would have sounded odd to some of Mackenzie King's later political enemies and victims: "His major weakness, I believe, was a high virtue gone to excess: his considerateness toward friend and foe.   As a cub debater back in the 1890's, his speaking ability was marred by his conceding too much to his opponents, and so his side didn't always win."

The years at Berlin High School were precious to an incipient scholar and teacher, who had been hungry for cultural and spiritual sustenance for so long. When High School days were over he attended an Ontario Model School and went teaching near home. Unfortunately, he discovered almost immediately that teaching was an uncongenial occupation. His temper was soon frayed, and he became subject to severe attacks of asthma.

About this time there was a family convulsion and migration. Grandpa Shantz, having founded several Mennonite colonies in Manitoba, trekked much further west, and in the North West Territories, a few miles before the foothills loomed up, he discovered a rich tract of homestead country. He became the founder of Didsbury, about 1893. Many Mennonite families and younger sons of Waterloo County farmers "pulled up stakes" in Ontario, and pioneered in the new tract opened up by Grandpa Shantz. Among them were Andrew Weber, Ephraim's father, and his two younger brothers, Manasseh and Edward. Manasseh, in his reminiscences, wrote enthusiastically about the "deep black soil, grass knee-high, with creeks and rivers of clear running water, coal deposits, timber in the Foothills of the Rocky Mountains and along river banks, water-power from fast-flowing streams." There was free land a mile from his father's Didsbury location, three miles from the railway siding, and in a mood of distaste for Ontario schoolteaching and homesickness for his family, Ephraim left the East and filed on a homestead in the North West Territories.

Even at Didsbury he could not escape entirely from a pedagogue's duties. Early in the history of the pioneer settlement of Didsbury, there was a public meeting called by parents to establish a school district. The bachelors, smelling taxes ahead, outnumbered the parents and voted down the proposal. So, Mr. Weber wrote me, "the parents engaged me to teach in one end of the immigration shed (twenty feet by one hundred, built by Grandpa Shantz), after my brother had contrived a blackboard, and things called desks. My salary was ten cents per day per pupil *if present*. One father couldn't make it, so I accepted a grindstone and a window sash. He had two boys. I had three miles to walk to school through a faint trail with grass shoulders high and began teaching the day sopping wet. (Dew.)"

Before long other scholastic arrangements were made, to the great relief of Ephraim Weber. For several years, while he "proved up" on his homestead, he was reasonably content. He became a proficient rider, a great lover of saddle horses, something of a "broncho buster." In the high and salubrious climate of the Foothill Province his health improved greatly. The asthma disappeared. But once the homestead duties had been completed, the old unease and wanderlust returned. He found the North West too solitary, too far removed from the centres of learning and music and culture. Yet the only other possible occupation, teaching, filled him with aversion. He fell victim to a pipe dream indulged in by so many thousands of similarly situated young people. He liked poetry. He aspired to write it. He scribbled. Could he not make a genteel living, even if modest, by his pen? These stirrings and vague ambitions were seething within him during the final years of the nineteenth century and the early years of the twentieth. Apart from the evidence in the letters he wrote to L. M. Montgomery, there are a few revealing glimpses elsewhere.

A month before his first letter to L. M. Montgomery, in February, 1902, "baching it" at the time in his den within sight of the Canadian Rockies, he wrote thus to his own school chum Leslie Staebler (by now a westerner also, a piano teacher at Fernie, B.C.), in reply to an invitation to visit him: "As to my going to Fernie, I have decided to continue in my den until next November, doing some little work in our fields during the summer. I am direly short of dollars. My solitude has not oppressed me quite so much lately. I go out more, and besides I have two or three very nice literary correspondents, to whom I write many a lonely hour and thus enjoy myself exquisitely. Sometimes I'm so lost in literary heavens that my den seems, not a lumber shack built on Alberta rock, but a castle in the air. This morning, for instance, the sun without and the 'sun within' and the unworldly quiet make an ideal Indian summer in this retreat of mine. I can read and think and exult in here as I cannot do elsewhere." He was composing quatrains and concluded this letter as follows: "I am happy to know the quatrain is precious to you. I have re-written it:

THE WAY HOME

When lost upon the dark and snowy plains,
The rider to his steed confides the reins—
Till home-lights gleam! So I, great Father, try
My long wild world-way by faith's homing eye.

"The printed one reads:

THE THUNDER

A droning August languor dungeoned me
  In dusty littlenesses of my fate;
Then boomed God's thunder. Straight my soul limped free,
  And, lightning-beckoned, oped the eternal gate.

Faithfully yours,

Ephraim."

In July, 1902, he writes again to his old friend:

"My dear Leslie:

"I think of you oftener than I write. The evidence of genuine friendship is, I hope, the capability to live without much demonstration. We cannot delight each other so much as we once could in our similarity of plans for knowledge and examinations, but we are still interested in each other's little efforts toward our separate goals. There is not such an ocean of difference between the kind of music you're trying to put out upon the air and the kind of literature I'm struggling to find utterance for. These are twin-hints of the Infinite Beauty, while other arts are only cousins to these and to one another. Yes, genuine music and genuine literature are twin-revelations of the Something we have no language for. I know your talent to appreciate real literature, and I think you know mine to listen to real melody. Never yet have I escaped the deific ache when real harmony reached my ears. . . . Our literary society is still alive. I write very little. I read much. A writer must have been a student. When you are in my den I'll show you my tiny bit in print worth seeing."

Later on that year (1902), after expressing the hope that his old school friend is "developing into a West Canadian Liszt," he answers an unexpressed question about his own fortunes: "I? Getting lost in this elemental whacking. My ex-violin brother and I are trying to knuckle an existence out of the elements here. We [three brothers] are cooperating in the project of creating farms here out of the nothingness—and I have only two hands to co-operate. Things are so unorganized and the spaces so big that the day goes over us with little effected. I seldom retire to my den, and have to work out my salvation against husky frontier facts."

These facts and fragments of correspondence and reminiscence will, I hope, give the reader some insight into the personality of the "Ephraim Weber" who was to begin the forty-year exchange of letters with L. M. Montgomery in 1902.

VI

The correspondence began, it will be recalled, with L. M. Montgomery on the staff of the Halifax *Daily Echo* and Ephraim Weber in his homestead "den" three miles east of Didsbury. He is amazed that she finds time to write him "through such a diversity of interruptions as you describe, but I presume the marine editor keeps you animated and purposeful." He is glad to know she got as much as twenty-five dollars for a story. He apologizes for asking her how much the editors pay her for poetry. He hopes to earn something himself that way. He sends her the poem he wrote to accompany a parting gift of one thousand dollars from the "old boys" when J. W. Connor resigned from the headmastership at Berlin High School. He likes her nature rhapsodies and shares with her his own almost uncommunicable feelings on the infinite prairie. "Last night" he got lost on the range and gave himself up to nature with perfect abandon. "I was the night and the chinook and the grass and the horizon and the wild roses and Wordsworth and the frogs! I don't know how to talk about it. I was infinitely refreshed." Does she ever have such experiences? Is there any sense in his words? She has evidently told him, in a letter of April, 1902, that she is leaving Halifax to return to Cavendish. Will she then have more leisure and repose for writing? He wonders how she manages so much literary work—and such excellent work. "You work prodigiously; don't hurt yourself, dear friend." And he ends his May 10th letter with a benediction: "And now may the grace of Euterpe be plentifully with you, my dear lyrist." He receives a card in June saying that she is on her way to Cavendish, and becomes impatient to have a letter from her. He has read one of her recent sea poems. "The sea keeps you inspired. It gives you a semi-dramatic outlook. I wish I were near that mighty Shakespeare of God. Of course, I have the mountains. Far, far away, in the land of sunset, they loom up like great anticipations." He found her *Canadian Magazine* poem eloquent. Does she remember what she got for it? Too bad we have to go peddling our literary wares in Uncle Sam's cities. "We'll be dead long before Canadian literature will be a bread-and-butter affair."

Her eagerly expected letter from Cavendish arrives, and he writes back immediately from the den. So she's left her boarding house and grimy Halifax? "I'm glad you got home safely and that the blooming orchards were such an exquisite drink for you. The old garden must be 'a thing of beauty and a joy forever,' and I'm glad it did you so much good. Your description of it is engaging. Have you become sober yet from the lily fragrance?" So she lay in bed nearly all Sunday reading novels! "So Cavendish is a quiet dreamy nook. No wonder you want to be there, where old gardens, ancient orchards and the sea inspire you." He is much encouraged by her account of earnings from sales. "You've done exceptionally well, and here are my heartiest congratulations." He is inspired to tell her what poetry means to him. "The more I think over God and life and nature and salvation and everything, the deeper and more missionful does this art of yours and mine seem. It is a serious and profound undertaking to reach into the flying chaos of thought and emotion and bring out into black-and-white a hint of the Infinite, for whom mortals are thirsting so. . . . To me, God is a poet, and there is no poetry in which He is not." He gets a "passing whiff of the Creator" in her poem, "The Sea Spirit." "Will you let me call a poet a good conductor of God? Although I cannot nod to many things men prattle about God and his Book, of this I am quite sure—that He is waiting *to be conducted* to human hearts or human consciousness or whatever you'd have me call it. . . . It seems to me that if we live so that we can open our beings to deific influx, the spirit of utterance will awaken there from slumber. Really, Miss Montgomery, I believe there is inspirational pressure above us and that it will flood every bosom that opens its sluice gates." He apologizes for all this moralizing. He finds her stories interesting, but thinks that her poetry has more distinction. She writes back approving of his sentiments about poetry, but perhaps deprecates a bit his high moral seriousness on the matter. It might be good for him to be less idealistic about it, he grants, for then he might write more. One saying of hers "saves her" in his estimation. "It is that you write poems because it is your nature to—as the birds sing. Well now, this is sublime, whether your inspiration is conscious or unconscious." It beats him how she wrote "Sea Gulls" in a printing office! He tells her about Pauline Johnson's poetry recital in Didsbury. He is sad to hear that the *Canadian Magazine* doesn't pay for poetry. He is restless. "The fact is, I'm not living the kind of life I want to, and am in a transition stage from the old to the new." He likes new things, but isn't to be considered a reformer. What does she think of Whitman?

He tells her his own views. He thinks much of the old ways and creeds is obsolescent. He's even tolerant toward Christian Science. "The great variety of faiths shows me the infinity of God. What are your views?"

On September 26th, he says he has been a loafer in the hay meadows and harvest fields for the past month. He's been sorely perplexed of late whether to go back to teaching. There is a good demand and salaries are "pretty good." Still, he doesn't like teaching, and wants to get at scribbling. Teaching would be only a temporary stop gap. What does she think he might hope to earn by his pen? She counts on doubling her present earning ability in, say, five years more, doesn't she? That would be better than teaching, wouldn't it? So he hasn't seen her best prose? Is there no way for him to see it? Is she writing a novel? What is it doing in her scrap-book? He sees from her letters that the finding of subjects is an art. She is beginning to have a wide market before her.

On October 24th he has more of her literary work to discuss. He is aware that only a few can live liberally from the earnings of their pen. His ideal would be to get writing and easy out-of-door work into "harmonious juxtaposition." A man must be his own boss if he counts on writing. "I shall not teach again. I don't like the work." Prefers a bit of agriculture, which is not so antagonistic to the pen as teaching. "Religious problems interest me particularly, because I'm in a transition from the old thought and creed to some new and undefined life."

Meantime Miss Zieber has been enjoining him, virtually ordering him, to come to Philadelphia, to be close to markets, and to make a serious effort at making a living by free-lancing. On November 25th, he reports he is to start east "the day after tomorrow," and would have left earlier only that he has had to borrow the money against his land, and the legal transaction has taken longer than he expected. "Many thanks for your cordial wishes for a pleasant winter in Philadelphia. Don't you wish you could join us?"

The next note is from Philadelphia, and for the next eight months his letters are filled with detailed accounts of his life there, his friendly relations with Miss Zieber, his unsuccessful assaults on the magazine market, Miss Z's equally vain efforts to make a living by writing, the handicaps he has to face, his deteriorating health (asthma again), the high cost of living in Philadelphia. He reads much in the libraries, attends church services in French and German, goes to band concerts, quartet recitals and choral performances. He comments on L. M.

Montgomery's expanding sales and enhanced receipts. "It's a caution how *you* fish up subjects." He deplores his ineffectual life. "I'm only a genteel tramp." (In a contemporary letter to Leslie Staebler he confesses that his earnings in the eight months at Philadelphia were only about thirty-seven dollars.) He begins to be homesick for the mountains and the high pure air of Alberta. He visits Philadelphia editors seeking to push his sales.

On March 31st he has just received an inspiring letter from her at Cavendish. "The poet was prime minister in the realm of being when you wrote me this latest letter. I was delighted. Give me Canada after all." They discuss Sunday Schools, and the Bible. "What you say of your experience of Sunday Schools is unfortunately also true of my own case. Still, I know the bare text of the Bible better than if I had not gone to that institution, all my life. I taught a class for fourteen years. We must now begin anew to read the 'wonder-book.' As literary pabulum it is fine; as a book of altruism and ethics it is all gold; as an inspired record of revelation and a means of spiritual salvation it may be the greatest of all literature, but I wonder how much of it is final and absolute truth. The human element is so evident. Perhaps a millennium hence a new Bible may be needed and therefore given."

On May 21, 1903, he responds to her nature rhapsodies. "I always delight in your descriptions of your rambles. Nature can solace when learning, art, religion and the world are only a weariness. Yes, flowers and trees and birds must be in their own wilds to have the highest beauty. You spin dear fancies about your favourite haunts."

On July 15th he acknowledges news of another L.M.M. triumph. "You've reached the gates of Mecca, I believe. Ever such hearty congratulations . . . on you going to get into *McClure's*. You'll alchemize your name by this. And what a push it will give you internally—interiorly! Did you spend much time and labour on this 'Romance'?" He will postpone replying to "the religious part" of her letter. "Much to think along that line."

On August 20th there is more good news to acknowledge. "Yours of July 30th was an inspiration to us for its facts and figures. We are ever so glad you are succeeding so beautifully, and thank you for letting us know all about it. A noble record it surely is. The serial is an achievement." She can certainly work marketability into her material. Philadelphia is a poor place for writing in the summer. He is going to New Hampshire in about six weeks. If he had money, Philadelphia could be home, but he'll go back to the country to wear out his old clothes. "I am essentially of the country anyway." So she would have a law against sad endings. "Oh I wish you could get one against sad endings in *life*!"

On September 21st he is still in Philadelphia. Is much impressed by her report that she received sixty dollars for the *McClure* story. "Whiw!" "My most exquisite congratulations to you. To what do you ascribe your popping success? Talent and hard work? What a momentum you'll gain from this achievement. Really, 'nothing succeeds like success.' We are proud to know you." He is desultory, but his life "is at present out of joint." On October 2nd he is to go to New Hampshire.

His next is from Cheever, New Hampshire, not far from the White Mountains. He is staying with a Joseph Goodfellow and his wife. Beyond the fact that Mr. Goodfellow was a Scot by birth and a graduate of Queen's University the correspondence yields little information. Mr. Goodfellow was a Greek and Latin scholar, and Mr. Weber regarded him as a severe but highly competent literary critic. Mr. Goodfellow was farming while he got ready to write and translate. He is "not easily satisfied, keen to see and ready to enjoy any good stroke of good work. Three-fourths of my stuff is no good he thinks—as I also do, but the other pitiable fourth, he says, is my justification and salvation." Goodfellow is complimentary about L.M.M.'s poetry. So she has already been asked by some publishers for a bunch of her poetry?

In a letter just after Christmas he discusses more of her literary work, including the serial which she has sent him. "Our Canadian periodicals appear to regard contributions to their pages as acts of patriotism, certainly not as business deals. $8 from *Canadian Magazine* for a story!"

By March 21st he is on his way home to Alberta. He writes from Berlin, from his old native haunts, having lingered in Rochester and Buffalo two or three weeks on his way west from New Hampshire. It isn't much of a letter, he confesses. "I'm letting my letters get shabby to you. Don't write a good letter, for I don't deserve it."

May 2nd finds him reestablished on the prairie. "I had the grip for a week, and now except for blistered hands, blistered feet, twitching muscles, aching bones, lame back, gnawing hunger, weariness, homesickness for civilization—I feel first rate. I'm just back from a chase after the cattle. I've been plowing, painting rooms, and milking." On June 25th he acknowledges hers of May 31st (1904). "I like your generous plentitude in your correspondence. Have you many regular correspondents? My 30 or 32 are about equally divided, Canada—U.S., one in Scotland." Her notes are getting to have "the majesty of real authorship. Say, do your neighbours know what you are doing? I'm delighted at your cash and prestige. . . . You'll soon be hired on a salary by the year to write for the Cook [publishing] house."

On August 20th rain has stopped the haying so he has the pleasure of writing her. How do you manage all your correspondents? One in Germany? Has read her trade notes three times. "You are having steady growing success because you have built up solidly from the bottom."

On October 4th he is very glad that she loves her "moonsprees" so, and that she gathers the souls of the flowers to bless her winter life. "Yes, I also have never wished heaven to have no night, and the revelator [St. John] judged all humanity by himself when he rejoiced over a nightless paradise. He no doubt dreaded night in his houseless life on bleak Patmos. I fear that the inspired fellows often revealed as much of themselves as of the Almighty and the hereafter. Now frankly, don't you too? Certainly we need not be irreverent on that account; only we need be on our guard against taking the details too seriously, otherwise we shall fall into the ugly narrowness of literalism, Puritanism, Swedenborgianism or what would you have? Not that *you* need any such exhortation." He thanks her for snapshots of the Island. "It must be a homey place you have, very cheery and yet retired. Nature here is so tremendous and thin that we have to be content with the sweep of the elements. There are hardly any details here, and the prodigious centralities—space, frost, firmament, fertility, drouth, wind, heat and the almanac-despising seasons." He comments approvingly on the latest things of hers she has sent him. Says she can stand aside. It is the grace of humour, which sees itself almost as others do. Blessed are the fun makers. The Philadelphia visit was a wild goose chase. He is repenting in leisure in the sweat of his brow. "I was 10 months in Philadelphia and don't know what's going on—and went 2700 miles to get there, and for no purpose but to widen my life, my narrow existence. It fractured my finances."

"Thank you for telling me in so many frank and generous words that my letters are worth getting," he stresses. "I'm ashamed I let you get ahead of me in this." Now it looks like mere politeness for him to say that he enjoys her letters. "But I

trust you to believe it is a sincere statement.   I write such long
and frequent letters to few.   I like your candid, sincere, fireside
style of letter.   You are always so jovial and steady, and you
don't cramp the spirit of your letters by replying to all the details
of mine.   I'm glad you are a Canadian."   This was much the
longest of his letters to date, occupying fourteen closely written
pages, or about 4,500 words.

VII

For the years 1905 to 1909 the letters from L. M. Montgomery were, with a few exceptions, preserved by Mr. Weber.
They are allowed here to tell their own story, with a minimum
of notes or comment from the editor.   I have attempted,
however, by a series of short links between the Montgomery
letters to bring out as completely and vividly as possible the
flavour and significance of her comments.

The first letter from Cavendish is dated March 7, 1905, and
is in direct reply to a letter from E. Weber dated January 19th.

Three pages of his January letter tell about an expedition to
the "Big Red Deer" River, in company with his dentist, who
owned a coal mine there, and wanted it surveyed, located and
described, and a trail blazed to it.   The long trip began just
before New Year's Eve.   They were benighted on the trail, and
thought they would have to spend the night in the open, walking
to keep warm, but at the last minute came upon a logging camp.
There, with thirty "bushwhackers," they celebrated the coming
of the New Year.   Later, in an abandoned shack near the mine,
they found a box of Grape Nuts, a fine new fur coat, a set of
harness and a pipe.   Mr. Weber speculates on the fate of the
owner of the cabin.   Another page is devoted to the story of the
loss of a favourite farm animal, a breed Belgian mare to be exact,
"young and liquid-eyed, a white star on her forehead" who
"looked intelligent enough to read a newspaper."   The Webers
had mortgaged one of their farms to buy this mare and its mate,
but "the other day she got her leg kicked to slivers" and though
they worked several days and nights to save her, "her agony
ever increased" and they were compelled to shoot her.   Do you
like horses? he asks L.M.M.   Have you ever loved one?

"I hope to hear of accepted stories, cheques, and sleigh
parties when you write again," he concludes his letter, "and if I
practise up, will you let me take you for a skate?"

The Letters

Cavendish, P.E.I.,
Tuesday,
March 7, 1905.

My dear Mr. Weber:—

I picked up a paper today and read therein that sowing had begun in Alberta! Then I looked out of the window and saw drifts 20 ft. high!!!

We have had a perfectly awful winter here. The like has never been known even by that mythical personage the oldest inhabitant. We thought last winter terrible but it was not so bad as this. We have had nothing but storm after storm, train blockages, and irregular mails. In short, our accumulation of ills reminds me of the story about an old Scotch settler who came home one night to find his house burned down and his wife and children murdered by Indians. He sat down amid the ashes of his home and said, "Well, this is perfectly ridiculous!"

Surely, however, the worst is over now. They used to teach us in school that March is a spring month!

I went away from home for a visit early in February, just after your letter came and did not get back until a week ago. I've been trying to "catch up" ever since.

I, too, received a postal from Miriam at Xmas, saying that she would write me "*immediately* after the New Year." However, no letter has yet come to hand; her definition of "immediately" seems elastic. I envy her her Florida winter when I grow restless with my prison of drifts.

My principal amusement these days is prowling around up to my ears in snow with my camera. I have secured a lot of snow scenes, some of the big drifts, especially those in the woods are curious and beautiful in the extreme.

Oh, why don't you make "copy" of your adventures while looking for the mine? I'm sure there is material for a whole "shilling shocking" [sic] in that deserted shack with the fur coat! So you eat "Grape Nuts"? So do I and have 'em every morning for breakfast! Another taste in common!!

Am sure you must have felt badly over the loss of your mare. I can fully understand how anyone can grow strongly attached to a pet. I love horses, dogs and cats. As I'm situated now I can only keep a cat but I'd love to have *lots* of them all. The first *real* sorrow that ever came into my life was connected with the death of a pet. I was nine years old. I had a little grey kitten, a pretty playful little creature which I loved with the passionate intensity of a lonely child possessing no other companionship. My kitten died one day of poison. I shall *never* forget the agony I endured. I really almost went mad. I shrieked, writhed, wept, until the good people of the household verily believed me possessed. They could do nothing with me. It was my baptism of sorrow and I was submerged beneath those waters of Marah. I have never laughed, in maturer days, over that tragic bereavement. It was too real—and symbolical. I had learned what pain was—a lesson we can never forget. It was the Alpha of life's suffering. Before that I had been a happy, unconscious little animal. From that time I began to have a soul!

You asked me in your letter a question rather hard to answer. It was "Where do you feel most yourself, in the woods or up in Charlottetown?"

Well, I feel most like myself in both places—if you understand the contradiction. There are two distinct sides to my nature. When I go to the woods the dreamy, solitary side comes uppermost and I love the woods best. But when I mingle with other people quite another aspect rules me. I am very fond of society, sparkling conversation, the good *human* times of life. These tastes find indulgence in my city experiences and I feel just as much at home there as in the wilds. I can slip from one to the other as easily as I can slip from one garment into another.

But as to being only "*two* of me" as you ask—bless the man, there's a hundred of me. (Association of ideas! Have you ever read *Dr. Jekyll & Mr. Hyde* by Stevenson. It is well worth reading and enforces a strong lesson. If it ever comes your way read it.) *Revenons aux moutons!* Some of the "me's" are good, some *not*. It's better than being just two or three, I think—more exciting, more interesting. There are some people who are only *one*. They must find life as insufferable a bore as other people find them. By the way, have you ever read any scientific articles on the curious mental phenomena of "double personalities" or "double consciousness"? If you have, you will agree with me that they are very interesting and curious. But if you have not don't ask me to explain about it for I could not do so. I mean, it would require more of a technical vocabulary than I have at command as well as a clearer grasp of the manifestations of this strange thing.

I've been re-reading *Trilby* today. It is a favourite of mine. Have you ever read it? If so please tell me what you think of it. Such a storm of controversy raged about it when it came out first, about seven years ago. I talked about it with two ministers in the same day. Both were men whose critical opinions were worthy of respect. One said he thought it one of the most charming little stories he had ever read, so touching and pathetic, and said he had given it to his daughter to read. The other condemned it utterly saying it was "the canonization of the scarlet letter." For my own part I think it is a dear, delightful book, wherein some of my most beloved book-friends live. It ends up with some verses that I copied into my portfolio and read them every day. Here they are for you, if you don't already know them.

> "A little work—a little play
> To keep us going—and so good day.

> "A little warmth, a little light
> Of love's bestowing—and so good-night.

> "A little fun to match the sorrow
> Of each day's growing and so good-morrow.

> "A little trust that when we die
> We reap our sowing and so good-bye."

Don't dare to say you don't like them!!!

Tonight, coming home from a tramp over snowy hills I halted a moment to look over the orchard fence at my flower bed. Not that I could see much of it—it is heaped over with a snow-drift fifteen feet deep, gleaming in the twilight like a mausoleum of marble built over buried dreams.   What are my tulips and daffodils and peonies doing down under it, I wonder—the dear things.   My only consolation on some of those terribly stormy days this winter was to get out a flower catalogue and plan my next summer's garden!!

By the way, what do you think I got in the mail today, sent me by a friend in Scotland?   No less than a sprig of mountain tansy picked on the grave of the celebrated "Black Dwarf." Wasn't I proud?   A whole Scottish "loch" wouldn't [have] delighted me more.

I suppose you will wonder if I'm doing any writing at all just now.   Oh yes, I peg away a couple hours every day, and have had the usual run of moderate successes.   But I've made a discovery!   Nothing less than a really truly Canadian affair that opens its eyes and says "papa" and "mamma."

In January I had a letter from the editor of the "Sunday School Publications," Confederation Life Bldg., Toronto, Can., saying that they published three papers for young people of varying ages and asking me for stories.   I sent a short girls' story—about 2500 words—and got five dollars for it.   They pay regular rates and are especially anxious for Canadian contributions.   They publish sketches and essays also.   Write them for samples of the papers and try your luck with them.   They are very good papers, much the type of *Forward*.   I really didn't think we had anything so up-to-date in Canada.

I got into another new mag, *The National* of Boston, lately, with a short story.   It is to pay on publication.   It is a good second-classer.   Don't know what its rates are.

The Sunday School Times, your pet, sent me $6 for a poem "The Choice" recently.   Let me know if you see it when it comes out.   If not I'll send you a copy.

The C.E. *World* also took a poem and sent $4 for it.   This is the first time I've got into it with poetry.

I made *nearly* $600 last year—$591.85 to be exact. Shan't be content till I reach the thousand mark though.

I got a *Lippincott* today—the March no. Don't know why they sent it. Thought at first it must be because my verses were in it but they weren't. Do you see it regularly? If so please keep a lookout for them as I want to know when they appear. I have just started this sheet to say bi-bi on, because I'm out of "nerve." So will just say it and stop.

Yours sincerely,

L. M. Montgomery.

P.S. I believe you asked me to go skating with you. Sorry, but I can't skate. Never had a chance to learn somehow. Ta-ta all the same.

L.M.M.

P.S. No. 2. I received the *Outlook* you sent and enjoyed it very much. Thanks! Do you want it back? If so, I'll return it. If you have the March *Lippincott* read "The Second Nocturne of St. Patrick" if you want a good laugh. I think I've discovered why the mag. was sent to me. There is a "Walnut" in it by a friend of mine—Lucy Lincoln Montgomery—and she probably sent it to me. Did I ever tell you about her?

L.M.M.

"Indeed, that was an experience of life when you lost your darling kitten," Mr. Weber *wrote back on April 9th. "I have been reflecting upon what you said at the close of that story—'Ever since then I have had a soul.' It seems that our very souls, like our bodies, are born into consciousness by pain. Isn't it fascinating to think of the mysterious ministry of pain? What power and joy we owe to its various kinds!"*

He has been reading Souvestre's Philosophe sous les Toits *and considers it a "find." "I have never met a man in life or fiction whom I know better or love more than this* philosophe." *And this leads him to "offer a speculation on the translation of language. . . . It seems to me that only the intellectual part of a language—that which conveys knowledge—can be effectively and accurately translated. The soul of a language is too elusive for capture by foreign idiom. It reposes largely in verbal melody. Now this is the first thing destroyed and only partially restored in translating. Then what about the Bible? Are its translations perfection of Revelation? Is a reproduced text worth splitting the churches over? It seems to me that if the Bible were intended as anything more than a supplement to God's revelation of himself in life and nature, it would be written in, not translated into, every language, especially into such a language as English. Besides, it is the Bible of one people—the Jews. Even the New Testament is full of conceptions and literary inventions that are foreign to us, and which we have to try to appreciate. . . . I am sure you will not run away with the notion that I have no reverence for the Scripture and have become a disciple of Ingersoll or Voltaire. It is a gathering of authors of all degrees of inspiration, and of marvellous interest for those who are capable of serious emotion. Think how remotely it has come down to us, and how it reaches our heart of hearts. However, when the human mind—which is God-given as well as the Book—almost involuntarily enquires into things, the Book is certainly too interesting to be left out. This particular side of the subject I relished discussing with you more than with anybody I have the privilege to meet at present; but I fear I have strained the proprieties by generalizing so in a letter."*

Cavendish, P.E.I.

Monday Evening,

May 8, 1905.

My dear Mr. W.:—

I've been painting and housecleaning all day and have expended so much grey matter in the process that I'm afraid I haven't very much left for a letter. Nevertheless, I'll "do my best" and, as used to be stated in the copybooks of childhood "angels can do no more." Isn't it rather nice to know that there is at least one particular in which we can all be angelic. By the way, what is your conception of an angel?

(Perhaps it is taking an unfair advantage of a fellow-creature to fire off such a question at you on the second page of a letter when in the nature of things you'd still be looking for introductory platitudes.)

I hope that some day the man or men who are responsible for *my* conception will be given over to my hands, if so be that they still live. I refer to the people who drew and published the pictures of angels which used to adorn the Sunday-school papers of my childhood. When I think of an angel I can't help seeing one of those pictures—a creature wearing a sort of nightgown with big goosy(?)-looking wings branching out from their shoulders and a mop of untidy hair streaming over their backs. I should like to think of angels as Marie Corelli does—creatures shaped of rainbow light, but I can't. Those impressions of susceptible childhood are too strong.

At the present moment I'd rather be a girl than an angel if angels can't have mayflowers. I'm surrounded with them—mayflowers, I mean. A vaseful on each side of me and a big jugful on the shelf over my head. Oh, they are divine! A lot of us went up to the barrens Saturday and picked great basketfuls. Today I read that Henry Ward Beecher said once "Flowers are the sweetest things God ever made and forgot to put souls into." But I don't believe He forgot! I believe they *have* souls. I've known roses that I expect to meet in heaven.

Oh yes, yes, spring *has* come. You can't imagine how glad I was to see it. We had such a *terrible* winter. It was like being born again to see the drifts go and the catkins bud on the willows. I know exactly what I shall feel like on the resurrection morning! And I'm gardening, too. Three weeks ago I went out amid slush and took the spruce boughs off my tulip and daffodil bed. I didn't expect any of them would be up so soon—but when I lifted the boughs there were the dear green spikes up two inches. I felt just like a prayer when I saw them! There are big buds on them now and they will be out in full bloom in a week. It's lovely to be out poking into the moist earth again. In regard to your thoughts on the ministry of pain; yes, I agree with you in regard to one kind of pain. There are two kinds, don't you think! The pain God sends to us and the pain we bring on ourselves; the former is the fire of heaven, the latter the flame of hell. God's pain is indeed one of his ministering spirits. Great mysteries of soul-birth and soul growth are bound up in it and if we have the courage and the endurance to make a friend of it it will bring great gifts to us. But the pain we bring on ourselves through folly or wilfulness or even simple blindness! Ah, it is horrible; it is degrading; there is no fine,

high ministry in it; it burns and scars and defaces for our punishment.   The child whose father punishes it justly will be the better
for that punishment; but if it picks up a red-hot coal in its hand
its suffering will *not* better it—only make it a little wiser perhaps
with the sorry wisdom of experience.

Perhaps you are one of the fortunate ones who never picks
up red-hot coals—whose only knowledge of pain is taught by the
suffering God sends.   If so, you won't feel the truth of some of
these remarks.   I'm not; I'm always picking up the coals because
they sparkle and look pretty.   And then come the blisters!

.   .   .

I agree with you that all literature should be read in its own
tongue.   Much *must* be lost in translation—all the subtle shades
of meaning which go back to the very root-words of the language.
Its body may be translated but, as you say, its soul is lost in
the transition.   The coarser meaning may be expressed; the finer
cannot be.

As for the Bible, the same limitations must apply to it.
You know to be frank, I do *not* look upon the Bible as a book
inspired *by* God.   I look upon it as a book much of which is
inspired *with* God—a collection of the myths, history, poetry,
ethics and philosophy of a singularly spiritual (taking into
account the period in which they lived) people whose superior
conception of the Great Intelligence fitted them to be the mouth-
pieces of that Intelligence.   The Jews made a specialty of religion
as the Egyptians of architecture, the Greeks of literature or the
Romans of war.   As a result they were pre-eminent in it.   Their
conception of God was naturally marred by the errors of all
human conceptions of the Inconceivable.   But still it remains as
great and wonderful and striking as the rock-temple of Ipsambul.
There have been finer, nobler, more truthful conceptions since.
But that does not affect the grandeur of it, in contrast to the
reeking idolatry of the nations which surrounded them.

I read a very fine book recently by Newman Smith, *Through
Science to Faith*.   He leaves revelation entirely out of the question
and essays to prove a Directing Intelligence working towards a
certain goal, and resulting immortality by the conclusions of

science alone. The book pleased me much. It is so sane, so guarded, so logical. If it were mine I would send it to you but it is only a borrowed book. Keep the title in mind and read it if you ever get a chance.

While I have drifted into this subject I'm going to ask you a very old question. Will you answer it frankly: "What think ye of Christ?" Don't be afraid to say what you think. I'll respond as frankly. Do you believe he was God incarnate? Do you believe he rose from the dead literally?

.   .   .

My mountain tansy was from the grave of the Black Dwarf. Don't you recall Scott's famous novel of that name? It was founded on fact. The Dwarf really existed and this tansy grew on his grave. I bought the novel recently to be able to paste the tansy on the title page!

.   .   .

I've been on a debauch of books for a fortnight. A long-delayed grist of books for our library arrived and I've simply read myself stupid and soggy over them. The best was Jack London's *Sea Wolf*—a powerful thing but revolting in some respects. He can write, that fellow.

Recently, gardening, housecleaning, etc. has pushed literary work to the wall. I must sober up from book-saturation, get work done and take up my pen again. Had a lot of acceptances lately, nothing worthy particular mention except the taking of a story by the Associated Sunday Magazines. This concern seems to be flourishing. At first they sent me only $25 for a story but this time they sent $40. The story was "The Schoolmaster's Love Letters" and is something of a new departure in style for me. For this reason will try and send you a copy of it when published if possible.

McClure's can hold on to a thing, can't they? Fortunately one hasn't to wait until publication for their checks.

I got into a new mag. lately, *The Pilgrim*, of Battle Creek, Michigan. It is a good affair and has good names in it. They took a short story to be paid for on publication.

No, don't give up writing; it's the best method of soul cultivation there is; even if you never published another thing the writing of it would bring you a beatitude.

I haven't heard from Miriam. Nor do I really wish to, now. Don't misunderstand me. I enjoyed my correspondence with her and was sorry it lapsed. But it has lapsed so long now that the old interest has died out and it seems to me rather impossible to get up a new interest should she re-open it—like rekindling an outburnt fire. The gap has grown too wide.

I must go now for some friends have called. Wish I could send you the scent of the mayflowers in this letter. Or of a pale pink tea rose that is nodding over my shoulder.

Yours sincerely,

L. M. Montgomery.

Mr. Weber answered the foregoing letter on May 28th. He refused to flinch at her question, "What think ye of Christ?" though he admitted he had never before been faced quite like that with such a serious question: "I feel its weight and my unworthiness." Nevertheless he was "very glad" she asked it. His answer ran to three closely written pages. The heart of it lies in the following passage: "In the name of sincerity and reverence, and in the name of the involuntariness of belief, I confess I can't take Christ into my intellect or my heart as the Son of God. The startling doctrine that the Holy Ghost fulfilled the function of paternal originator seems too much like Oriental phantasy to enter into the life of us of the prosy New World and of another age." It would grieve his mother and some of his relatives and acquaintances to know his attitude on this point "—and I hate to grieve anybody." What would such people do if their old evangelical faiths were disturbed? "What could I offer them instead?" He wished he could believe that Jesus was actually the son of God as much as the son of Mary. "Don't you?—if you doubt it? What an ideal that would be! The old evangelical idea of the new birth is really most sublime, but the 'revival' people have made it immedicably morbid for me—as those frightful wings have spoiled the angels for you, and for me too." Isn't it stunning, he goes on, to reject a faith so sacred and so world-wide and so age-old? "It makes me feeble to think of the inconceivable magnitude of an idea that spreads and deepens into a belief like this. But I can't accept it. Perhaps I can some day—some great happy day. A man can't help his belief to suit the fashion. In the meanwhile I am trying to derive some salvation from his life, rather than from his death, and from his character—not from his blood, except in so far as it shows his character."

He wrote briefly again on June 15th, to say he had just seen her "Schoolmaster's Letters" in a Philadelphia magazine, and thought it the best thing of hers since the "Persian Kitten." He wondered if she was conscious where or how she got the idea for the story.

Cavendish, P.E.I.,
Wednesday Evening,
June 28, 1905.

Dear Mr. W.:—

I think your Alberta snowstorm in which you got caught has arrived here. Not that it is exactly snowing but it is almost cold enough to. We have had a dismal two days' northeast storm of wind and rain and my religion is at present Calvinistic to the back bone. I feel exactly as the old lady did who said, "The Universalists think all the world is going to be saved but *we Presbyterians hope* for better things!"

I'm down here by the kitchen fire because my den is really too cold to be comfy. I can't even get out to see my garden the orchard grass is so dripping wet.

The tulips are gone. I cut the last one yesterday. They were lovely while they lasted. There is nothing out just now; it's a sort of betwixt and between time; but there are lots of buds of roses, lilies and peonies. You ask what is my favourite flower. The carnation; and of carnations the pink carnation. I was in town last week and bought a couple of dozen cut carnations to bring home with me. I've just been revelling in them ever since. They combine perfect beauty of form and colour with perfection of perfume, to a degree that only the rose, and not always the rose, can rival. You say you don't like a bouquet which has no white in it. Well, I don't like *bouquets* at all in the sense of several varieties of flowers being bound together. I never mix flowers and very seldom colours. In a tall glass vase or low bowl, as suits the flower, I put a few blossoms of one kind with a bit of foliage or fern and then sit back and adore them. At the most I never put more than *two* kinds together. More would swear at each other, seems to me. You like the red rose best? I don't quarrel with your taste. I can quite understand a person liking red roses best. I don't, simply because I don't fancy red as a colour in anything except nasturtiums. The pink roses are my favourites—deep pink at heart, shading to almost white on the outer petals like a blush dying away. We have an old-fashioned hardy June rose in our garden here, a pink one, which for purity of colour surpasses anything I ever saw. It is only semi-double and loses its beauty when fully expanded but its half open buds are things to thank God for.

.   .   .

Glad you liked "The Choice." No, I didn't invent the metre. Saw it somewhere and fancied it. It is effective but hard to handle on account of the triple rhyme and the accent falling on the first syllable of the rhyme. Don't ask me to label the metre! I couldn't if I tried. I don't know a *solitary thing* about the names of metres. When I begin to write a poem the words seem to fall naturally into the rhythm best suited to the idea and I just *let* them fall and devote my energies to hunting out rhymes which I do in a very mechanical and cold-blooded way, using a little rhyming dictionary I made myself. (Tennyson used a rhyming dictionary you know. How nice to be like him in something!!) Sometimes I write a whole poem without a single rhyme in it. Then, when I've caged my ideas I substitute end words that rhyme and there you are!

What do you think! I got a letter from Miriam today. Everything comes to those who will but wait. I was glad to hear from her. The letter was very Miriamesque. I must answer her soon although I feel rather out of touch with her as a correspondent. She wrote quite frankly upon the subject of her marriage but, unless she has also written so to you, I shall not discuss it as she probably meant it to be regarded as confidential although not explicitly saying so. She seems to be happy with a decent, non-rapturous workaday happiness that isn't such a bad thing as the world goes.

.   .   .

Thank you for your frank answer to my question of the Christ. I share your views. I'd like to discuss the matter but it's too big a subject to be handled by letter. I never say much about it to anybody. Like you, I *cannot* accept the *divinity* of Christ. I regard him as immeasurably the greatest of all great teachers and as the son of God in the same sense that any man inspired of God is a son of God. Further than this I cannot, as yet at least, go. I believe that He was truly sent from and of God, as are all great teachers. And possibly he may also stand as an emblem of man in his highest and yet-to-be-attained development—the perfect flower of the tree of life blooming before its time as an earnest of what may be.

It seems to me that the discovery of the processes of evolution dealt the death blow to the old theology of Christ dying for Adam's sin. If man rose up from a lower form, as all scientists now agree, there was no "fall" and consequently no need of any "sacrifice" to square God and man.

The idea that Christ must have been a wilful imposter if he were not divine does not disturb me. Even if the gospels, written 30, 50, 60 or 80 years after his death, give us his words and meaning correctly—a very doubtful thing in my opinion—it does not disturb me to believe that he, in common with most great teachers and reformers, had an element of fanaticism—for want of a better word—in his character. It seems to me that it is a necessary ingredient in a highly-organized, sensitive character to enable it to make headway against a brutal world and all its sins and follies. Without it, it could not stand against its foes.

But, as I have said, the subject is too big for a letter. I'll meddle with it no further—in bulk, at least. Now and then, I may jot down a detail or so, as it occurs to me.

I received your second letter the very day I got a couple of extra *Sunday* mags. that I had sent for, one of which I meant for you but didn't send it since you already had it. No, I don't remember where or how the idea came to me. When I come across an idea for story or poem—or rather when an idea for such comes across me, which seems the better way to put it—I at once jot it down in my notebook. Weeks, months, often *years* after, when I want an idea to work up I go to the notebook and select one that suits my mood or magazine. I found the germ of the "Letters" in an old Halifax note book, inscribed as follows "Man writes love letters to girl, not intending to send them. Jealous woman sends them. Girl loves him." That's all I know about it now.

I've been very busy all June, writing. Got a good deal done. *Gunters* Magazine, New York, a new concern, sent me $25 for a short story. I was surprised to get such a good price as I did not think the Magazine was any great shakes, judging by its contents.

The *National* sent $10 for story accepted last winter which is to be published in July. Will try to send you copy. The *Designer* sent $20 for a story and *Modern Women* $15. Their prices seem to be rising. What with a number of smaller checks here & there I picked up over $100 since June came in. Wish I could do as well every month but there's generally a famine after a feast.

This sheet is started just to say good-bye in a decent space. I shall not try to spread any ideas over it. Good luck and good cheer, comrade.

Fraternally yours,

L. M. Montgomery.

There is a gap of nine months between the third and fourth letters from L. M. Montgomery as printed here. The gap represents three more lost letters. Mr. Weber answered hers of June 28th on July 30th; she replied about August 24th; he wrote again on September 24th, and was answered some time in November. He wrote twice in December—once on the 17th and again just before Christmas. She replied to these two early in the New Year, and he wrote back on March 3rd. The next letter from her, printed below, is in reply to this last. The discussion about Christianity continued. L.M.M. wondered if E.W. had read Renan's Life of Jesus. *She evidently assured him that her ideas about Christ were not echoes of someone else's beliefs.* "I too have been led to my views on Christ's divinity or non-divinity simply on my own hook," *he wrote in September.* "All my upbringing was wholly orthodox. But a man can't help his belief. As to my creed—I've never asked myself to *state it, but it would sound something like this: I believe in God's existence and his goodness, and that no virtue, no goodness and beauty exists disconnected from him; that in his economy no pure motive, no worthy action, no touch of love will be lost or crippled in the tangle and scuffle of things; that no bad impulse and unbrotherly thought will escape punishment in this life. But I can't get it down. I might as well say, God is love and things are going to come out right."* On December 17th he mildly complained that her latest letter was "the first one that wasn't first rate since our correspondence opened—and that's quite a record." He told her about selling his farm and buying another one since his last letter. One of his brothers had been "married off," and his parents were retiring into a new house the family had built that summer in Didsbury. On an impulse he had sold his own homestead with the intention of going away to the cities and making his living at some semi-literary vocation, but he found himself more deeply rooted into the soil of "Sunny Alberta" than he had realized. She had asked him for a contribution to the Cavendish Literary Annual. He had tried several times to compose something, but "to save my soul, I couldn't get anything worth reading together." He was startled at his inability to sit down and write, and asked for her counsel, what should he do? They discussed eternal life, Nirvana, reincarnation. He reported his reactions to Ruskin. "He reminds me now of some of our old timers who are out of patience with current modes. . . . Ruskin lacks humour." He is pleased she's reading Shakespeare. "Our Shakespeare class is just finishing *Julius Caesar* and commencing *Macbeth*." "I'm still in true Western jack-of-all-trade degradation," he ends his letter. "Today I worked in a stone quarry; yesterday I was auctioneer's clerk; day before I was driven out by the real estate fellows in search of land; tomorrow I'll help to dig father's well. Good night. Your sincere friend, Ephraim Weber."

Cavendish, P.E.I.,
Sunday Evening,
April 8, 1906.

My dear Mr. W.:—

I've just roused up from a long twilight visit to my castle in Spain. For the past hour I have been lying on a couch in my den beside a dying fire—that is, my *body* was lying there but my soul was far away in a dreamland of imagination, where everything lost or missed in my present existence is mine. What a blessing it is that we can so *dream into* life the things we desire! Are you too an owner of a Spanish castle? And how often do you let yourself visit your estate? I go there in the twilight, being too busy at other times to remember my duties as Chatelaine. Outside, it is a cold, blustery April rain, the air all mist the ground all mud. But in fancy I've been far away beyond the mud and mist to "cloudless realms and starry skies."

Now for your letter.

Yes, our Literary Society paper—the *Cavendish Literary Annual*—came off on schedule time and was fairly good, though we—the editors—"say it as oughtn't." We had a number of contributions from various writers, one all the way from Scotland so our table of contents was quite cosmopolitan.

I was concerned at what you said about your inability to write. Surely you've let yourself drift into dangerous shallows. Perhaps you are spending *too much* time in your castles in Spain! If so, adopt my plan—seek them only at twilight or midnight and accept your exile at other times. There is no power that so speedily rusts as that of expression. *So to work at once, stick to it,* write something *every day*, even if you burn it up after writing it. Otherwise you'll atrophy to a certainty. There! I hate giving advice as cordially as I hate taking it. I'm glad that's over!!!!

My flowers are all done—the daffodils and hyacinths at least. But I've some house roses coming out and a big Easter lily. I've been coaxing the latter along with an eye to next Sunday and I think it is going to be out in time. I'm expecting great things of it for it was a big bulb and has grown thriftily.

Oh, yes, it *is* fascinating to suppose that we go from one existence to another, with the restful sleep of so-called death between! To me, the idea is a thousand fold [more] attractive than that of the Christian's heaven with its unending *spiritual* joys. I'd rather *life as it is in this world*, accepting all its ups and downs, its sorrows and pains for its joys and delights, than such. Besides, even the ideas of people who call themselves devout Christians about heaven are almost ludicrously vague and shapeless—and they don't seem to find the prospect especially inviting either. At least, they never seem in any hurry to go there—far from it. And how illogical they are. For example: I was recently talking to a middle-aged woman who had lost a young sister from death. She said "it was so sad to see a young person die, *without having lived their life.*"

Now, if that woman had believed that there was no future life her remark would have been just and logical. But she believes—or would tell you she believed—that her sister had gone straight to heaven and that she was much better off and that heaven was a much happier place than this world. Now, if this were a sincere vital belief with her why should she or anyone regret—on behalf of the dead person, I mean—that the life had not been fully lived here! It *does* seem to me that the instinct of humanity thus gives the lie to the conceptions of the theologians. I have not made my meaning particularly plain in all this. I hope you will be able to grasp the idea in spite of its clumsy presentation. These subjects, however, cannot be well discussed by letter. They demand personal contact where objections etc. can be stated and discussed at once.

I agree with you that sunflowers seem masculine, and I would add another. To me the common red clover of our hay fields always seems masculine. The fine white or faintly tinged pink clover is a little lady but the big chubby red clovers are sturdy country lads.

No, I've never heard from Miriam. She did not even acknowledge the little booklet of verse I sent at Xmas but she may not have received it. By "faring passably well" do you refer to her health or her circumstances. She was suffering much from rheumatism when I last heard from her.

No, I don't think I can define what it is that Ruskin lacks, although I feel it acutely. I admit all his good qualities. But then

If (s)he be not fair to me
What care I how fair (s)he be,

to mis-apply an old couplet very illustrative of human nature. Perhaps, as you suggest, it is a sense of humour. He does take himself so terribly in earnest over things that are only of secondary importance after all. In one of his books, *Beauty and Nature*, he says some exquisite things about the sky for which I could almost find it to give him a place in my heart.

Thank you for the *Cosmopolitan* and Markham's poem. I enjoyed it with qualifications. It possesses great beauty—but it is the secondary beauty of complexity not the primary beauty of simplicity.   I don't altogether understand your question marks. Do you mean that you disagree with the ideas expressed or disapprove of the method of their expression?

I don't like his calling her *Virgilia*—which is a Roman name—when the whole spirit of the poem seems to throw it back to a primal time of earth's childhood before Rome or even Egypt had a name.   His ideas don't seem to be especially well connected—I think he sometimes sacrifices sense to rhyme. Then in his fourth verse

> One afternoon the stars were slipping
> Pearl after pearl to the bowl of night

rather pointedly suggests Omar's lines

> Morning in the bowl of night,
> Has flung the stone that puts the stars to flight.

The line

> To turn from love is the world's one treason,

is good and true when taken in the widest sense.   On the whole, I liked the poem, got pleasure from its perusal and thank you for sending it.

By the way, a literary correspondent of mine in New York writes me that he has a personal acquaintance with Markham and that the latter is suffering from "swelled head."

I've been scribbling away.   Had a story in April *Gunters*. Will send you a copy by and by if possible.   I haven't been paid for it yet but I got $25 for a former one there.

I enclose a copy of my verses in a recent number of *Lippincotts*.

The *American Home* recently sent me $18 for a short 3,000 word story.   This is surprisingly good pay for such a concern. Their price is *ten cents a year*.   You remember I sold them a serial once.   Last week I got a letter from them urging me to write them an 18,000 word serial.   So I'm trying to do it and have almost got it done.   It's a sensational tale about a lost ruby and I shall be ashamed of it but shall expect a liberal check.

Over a year ago I wrote an article, "The Old South Orchard." It wasn't a story but just a sort of essay relating fictional incidents about an old homestead garden. I sent it to the *N.Y. Xian Advocate* which acknowledged. As time went on I flattered myself it was accepted—as that is their method usually —and as good as credited myself with the usual $5 check. Just a *year* from date of sending it came back without a word of explanation or apology. I was furious and meditated sending a sarcastic note to the editor suggesting that he expurgate the word *Christian* from his paper's name. However, I calmed down and sent the MS to *Outing*, New York. Yesterday I got a letter offering a cent a word (about $40) for the article and asking for more like it. The editor said he admired its "fine simplicity" and wanted to know if I had any intentions of working material up into a book, as the Outing Co. published books etc. *Outing* is a fine magazine and I'm tickled over the outcome and quite ready to bless the *Xian Advocate* man for his unintentional good turn.

The Churchman, New York, is paying good rates now. Sent me $9 apiece for a couple of 2000 word kid's stories.

Recently I've been dipping into history and am reading Gibbon's *Decline and Fall*. Last night I read his two famous chapters on Christianity. He impressed me as having attained perfection in the art of saying one thing and meaning the very opposite. He defends and praises the Xian religion and every word is a subtle sneer. Have you ever read it? It's a massive work and makes me dizzy thinking of the amount of research and drudgery it must have entailed.

It's time to say goodnight. So consider it said.

Ever your sincere friend,

L. M. Montgomery.

His letter of May 5th told of a minor accident and its aftermath: "*I was in a sand pit. A chunk of ground caved in on me, knocked me over and pinned me fast by the leg. I was lame for ten days. Not able to do anything outside I betook myself to writing (short compositions for practice), languages (Latin, German, French, English), and literature*

(*Shakespeare, Bible, Cowper*); *and had such a nice time that I almost regret the fading of my lameness. . . . Did you have any MS in 'Frisco?" he continued, in reference to the severe earthquake there on April 18th. "One of my correspondents had several things, and no doubt they are destroyed."*

Cavendish, P.E.I.,
Thursday Evening,
June 21, 1906.

My dear Mr. W.:—

Your letter has been lying in my portfolio for over a fortnight waiting a chance to be answered. From this you would infer I was a very busy person, wouldn't you? Well, in truth I am. Not that I'm doing much worth while but I really seem rushed to death with a lot of little wretched duties that have to be done for peace' sake and eat up all the spare time. However, I've a breathing space tonight and I'm going to make the most of it. But it will be merely a scribble—not a letter.

I'm all played out! We had a Sunday School Convention in C. yesterday—a species of religious dissipation which beats a midnight dance all hollow for taking the stamina out of one. I feel tired down to my toes. For about eight consecutive hours yesterday I listened to reports, discussed methods, heard addresses, played in the choir, or sat up stiffly, dressed in my best and looked attentive. Some of the features were interesting —others bored me. All in all, I don't believe I shall be a whit the better Sunday School Teacher for it—and I'm sure I'm the worse Christian today! I feel positively impish and quite ready to persecute anyone who doesn't agree with me in creed!

Was sorry to hear of your accident but if it had as good an aftermath as you say perhaps it was well it happened and you ought to be congratulated rather than condoled with. Isn't it odd how often things like that turn out to be blessings in disguise, while on the other hand things seemingly desirable and which please us most mightily at first draw after them a train of most unrighteous consequences. Is it all a chance medley—or is it Providence?

Yes, my N.Y. correspondent is a literary man—Gerald Carlton, who has written a lot of novels. They are *not* literature —very sensational etc. But his letters are all right. He is an elderly man and a retired British army officer but an Irishman by birth. He is the personal friend of a personal friend of mine in Halifax and it was thus I became acquainted with him. He seems to have had a wide acquaintance among writers—knew R. L. Stevenson, Wilkie Collins and that set intimately.

I finished my serial and sent it to the *American Home*. I haven't heard from it officially yet but in a note from the editor about another matter he said he would report on the story soon and he thought the report would be favourable—a cryptic utterance that inspires me with hope.

Gunters sent me $35 for the "Education of Sally." I sent you a copy recently. They accepted another story last week and it is to be published in September. I've been doing a lot of work for juveniles and scooping in several checks of $8 and $10. In April the *Youth's Companion* took a poem and sent $12. They have four of mine on hand now, two of them for over two years. *Outing* sent $38 for my orchard article. Last week the *National* accepted a ghost story to be published in September, price $10. The *Housekeeper*, Minneapolis, accepted a story yesterday and sent a check for $25. This is a new place as I never landed them before. I've had a lot of my MSS. go astray this winter—never had such a time. I always keep a copy of course but the loss of time—and possible checks—is very annoying.

I had a letter from Miss C. last week. She, too, concocted a serial for *Am. Home* but hadn't heard from it.

I have invested in a new type writer. My old one, only a second-hand to begin with, was about worn out so I traded it off for a practically new one—an "Empire." It does fine work. But it has a different keyboard and so I have to learn all over again and I'm very slow. But this is a universal keyboard so when I do get expert at it I'll be able to write on any of the high-priced machines.

No, I had no MS in San Francisco. That 'quake was terrible. I suppose in a few weeks we will be inundated with stories of it and next year a whole flood of novels. Well, it would make a great subject—and require a great pen to do it justice.

Some callers have just come in. I must go down and as I will not have time to write any more tonight I'll finish this up although it is the merest apology for a letter. Next time I'll try to redeem my reputation.

Very sincerely yours,
L. M. Montgomery.

The above letter was answered on August 20th. Mr. Weber had meanwhile sent a "postal" to explain his delay. He was in the harvest rush, helping his brother get his 225-acre crop safely reaped and threshed. "I have been helping at various undertakings since mid-June, for he has 1120 acres of land . . . about a fourth of which is cultivated."

Monday Evening,
Seven O'clock,
October 8, 1906.

My dear Mr. W.:—

This is perfectly dreadful! But I *won't* apologize. I haven't had time, that is the simple fact. It seems almost uncanny that I have a spare hour tonight. Your letter has been haunting me like a reproachful spectre in the background of consciousness for weeks. Never mind, the long autumn and winter evenings are at hand and I shall behave ever so much better.

It has been awfully cold today and I've gone about with my teeth chattering. But we have had the loveliest fall, ever since the first of September—all purple and gold and mellowness in earth, air and sky.

Well, today I laughed until I cried. I only wish you had been handy to laugh too. You certainly would have laughed—or wept! Perhaps the latter would have been more fitting. It was certainly enough to make angels weep.

I received back a rejected MS. from *Lippincotts' Magazine.* This was not what I laughed over—or wept over either, being too well accustomed to that. But I thought it seemed much bulkier than it should so before putting it away in my desk I examined it and found that another MS had been returned with it—not mine, but, as the rejection slip showed, some Miss Richardson's of Philadelphia. I read it—and good heavens!

Anything like it I never heard of nor imagined. If I had not seen it "with my own eyes" I could not have believed that such stuff could ever be offered for publication in all seriousness—and to such a magazine as *Lippincotts* [at] that. Oh, I *wish* you could see it! Look here—you *shall* see it—you *must* see it! I'll send it to you in a separate parcel and you'll bless me forever for it. You can return it to me as soon as you've read it and I'll send it to the author. When you read it you will understand that delay is of no moment and you will also realize that my action in sending it to you justifies itself. If it doesn't kill you you'll enjoy it I think. I did, at least. Great masterpieces of humour have amused me less! Remember that this MS was offered in all seriousness to a first-rate American Magazine. I shall never growl at an Editor again. No matter what Editors do, they should not be blamed when they have to read such AWFUL stuff. It's a wonder they don't all have nervous prostration. Perhaps they *don't* read it though. Probably they never went beyond the first page of this. And yet the rejection slip was typewritten—said to be a mark of special favour!!!—while I got merely a printed slip. Probably the editor felt grateful to the author for a good laugh.

The American Home cashed up Saturday Oct. 6, after holding up my serial ever since last April. They sent me *eighty dollars* for it. It was fully all—and more—that it was worth for it was sensational trash. The last serial they bought from me, though of the same length, only brought in $40. It was about 20,000 words long and I wrote it in two weeks.

I have been home all summer. Last week I went to town for three days and had an enjoyable little outing. You say you wonder why I don't travel. It is simply because I cannot leave home.   Grandma is 82 and I cannot leave her, for even a week's cruise.   We live all alone and there is no one I can get to stay with her.   I am very much tied down but it cannot be helped. Some day I hope to be able to see a bit of the world.

I've been writing busily all summer, mostly it must be admitted, juvenile and S. School work.   I picked up enough ten and fifteen dollar checks to make it worth while.   *Holland's Magazine*, Texas, and *The Pilgrim*, Detroit, were two new places I got into.   The former paid $3 for a short 2000 word sketch and the latter promises ten on publication for a 3000 word story. I have done a good deal for *East and West* of Toronto.   They only pay $5 per story so I just send them second-rates.   Often they send me pictures and ask me to write stories to suit.   I *loathe* doing this—but still I do it!   The other day I had a letter from the *American Messenger* asking me for my photograph to be published among their contributors in their December announcement number!   The *Boy's World* asked me for four stories for 1907.   *East and West* also asked me to write a 6 chapter serial for them but I declined.   They would only pay $5 per chapter and in the same time I could write six short stories for American papers that would net $10 apiece.

Yes, I teach a Sunday School class—but I don't like it much.   I have a class of half grown girls but they seem stupid and commonplace.   They never dream of asking a question, much as I have tried to induce them to, and all their idea of "studying" a lesson seems to be to learn the printed questions in the quarterlies off by heart.   I never can get them to give an answer in their own words and I don't believe they ever get one scrap of real good out of the lesson.   I have to follow the old traditional paths of thought & expression or I would get into hot water immediately.   Cavendish is wholesomely (?) old-fashioned and orthodox.

By the way, do you notice how that word "orthodox" is degenerating?   With the preceding generation it was a term of honour and commendation.   With ours, it is tinged with contempt.   With the next generation it will be a term of reproach. Even words have to follow the inevitable natural law of rise, perihelion and decline.

My N.Y. correspondent is, to speak frankly, not much account. I don't care for his letters very much. He is the personal friend of a personal friend of mine and that is how I "met" him. If he were any good I would try to arrange a correspondence between you and him but I assure you it would not be worth while. I think that, personally, he is a fine, upright, clean-minded man, but intellectually he is only a cipher and our correspondence is *not interesting*, that's all. He has known quite a lot of famous writers though and seems to make his living out of journalism, etc. No, *Outing* hasn't published my sketch yet—won't till next summer. I had a story in September *Gunters* but I haven't been paid for it yet. They are always slow. I'm always expecting them to smash up, they publish such trash.

I like my Empire typewriter very much. Yes, it's a visible machine and does excellent work. A "universal keyboard" means a keyboard common to all the standard machines—that is, the arrangement of letters, etc. is the same and if you learn to write on one you can write on them all. My former machine did not have this keyboard so that I had to learn all over again when I got my Empire. But I'm getting pretty "slick" at it now.

A caller has just come in and I must close though I had a few more things to comment on. What do you think of the spelling reform agitation and Roosevelt's action thereon? Have you read Upton Sinclair's *The Jungle*? If not, *don't*—if you ever want to eat sausages or canned goods again!! It is *hideous*, morally as well as physically!

Ever your friend,

L. M. Montgomery.

In his letter of October 31st, Mr. Weber said that he "had got good and ready to hear" from her. He expressed warmest gratitude for her letter when it did come. He ended his eight small handwritten pages with the report that he had taken a job for the winter as elevator man for the Alberta Pacific Elevator Company at Didsbury. "Work is mechanical, commercial and clerical—and therefore foreign to my temperament. But I like the convenience and the 8-hour day."

Cavendish, P.E.I.,
Sunday Evening,
December 16, 1906.

My dear Mr. W.:—

This is good weather for writing letters! As for sending them, that is a horse of another colour. We have a mail now just when the mailman can get along—every third day as a rule. Between times we have storms.

This is the evening of a very dull sleepy Sunday. We had no service near and couldn't have gone to it if there had been owing to last night's storm. I did start out after tea, grimly determined to do a constitutional; but had to give up and come back, the drifts proving too much for me. So I'll write letters tonight for my Presbyterian ancestors are so thickly snowed over that I don't think they'll be able to turn in their graves because of it.

I thought you'd have a smile or two over that MS I sent. I re-read it before sending it to its owner and I laughed until I nearly cried. Your definition of "incoherent grasshopperishness" expressed all that criticism could say of it. Had I been the editor of *Lippincotts* I think I'd have bought the story and published it in the Walnuts and Wine department. Certainly nothing could be funnier.

No, I haven't any flowers outside *now*. But I have some indoors. I have a lovely 'mum out—seven or eight great fluffy pale pink flowers out on it. The 'mum is a society lady, all frills and chiffons and languid grace. My bulbs are beginning to bloom too and I expect a continuance of them right through the winter. My Roman Narcissus and white hyacinths are out now. The latter are the sweetest things God ever made. They seem more like the souls of flowers than like flowers themselves. Yes, I like tall flowers too—and glowing deep-tinted riotous ones— and *every kind*. But I love best the flowers I coax into bloom myself, be they tall or small, white or rosy. It seems as if I were taking a hand in creation—giving life to those unsightly bulbs that hide such rainbow possibilities in their cores. Isn't

it strange how such ugly things can give birth to such beauty—
the old mystery of good, like a white lily, springing out of the
muck and mire of evil. It is possible that evil is necessary to
the blossoming of good, just as the dirty clay and foul-smelling
fertilizers are necessary to the unfolding of those blossoms!
There's a theological problem for you!

I smiled over one question in your letter. Do I do any
housework? Well, rather—about all that is done here. I like
it, too, except the rougher parts, and I'm very fond of cooking,
etc., etc.

Well, I must tell you my *great news* right off. I think I've
mortified the flesh sufficiently by holding it back till the fifth
page. Two weeks ago *Everybody's* accepted a short story of mine
and sent me *one hundred dollars* for it! It was about 5000 words
long and humorous. It had also been rejected twice, once by a
magazine that pays $30 per story and once by a magazine that
pays *ten*. Next? Of course I felt pleasantly tickled.

After this other successes seem small but I've got into
several new places. The *Blue Book*, published by the Red
Book Co. of Chicago, took a story for ten dollars. The *Housekeeper* (but I'd got into this before) paid $20 for an oft-rejected
story. The *Rural Magazine*, Chicago, accepted a rural story to
be paid for on publication. *Watson's Magazine* New York sent
$10 for a poem lately. I never got more than $5 or four from
them for a poem before, but this was a long Christmas one.
So far this year I've made over seven hundred dollars.

Did you ever read a children's fairy tale *Through the Looking
Glass*? It's quite a classic in its way and the most delicious
nonsense. One of the characters has by long practice become
able "to believe seven impossible things every morning before
breakfast." But this faculty is not confined to the "Red Queen,"
I imagine, judging from the beliefs some people entertain!

I haven't got hold of many new books of late. One of the
few was *The Future Life* by a noted French writer. It was
interesting but not at all conclusive and left me with the conviction that the author, great scientist and all as he is, doesn't
really know a thing more about the future life than I myself

know—or than anybody else knows for that matter. Argument
or evidence can't prove it—only the soul speaking in us can
assure us of its own immortality. But in what shape is that
immortality to be! Will *I* be *I*? Isn't it strange—the horror
with which we shrink from the thought of losing our individuality?
Total annihilation would be preferable to becoming anybody
else, even though that anybody else might be a hundred-fold
better and nobler than ourselves.

Lately I've been thrashing out a new conception of life
after death but so far I haven't got to the stage where I can
express it clearly in words. I don't mean that it's a *belief*—no,
no, merely a theory. I don't think I have really any *belief* in
any particular kind of a future life. I believe that there *is* life
after death, that's all.

I have nothing more to say. Since the first of November
I've hardly been out of our own yard—never once more than a
mile from home. The weather last month was all rain—this
month it's all snow. So I'm going to cut this letter right off here
and now. Thanks for your last picture postal. Best wishes
for the Xmas season.

Yours sincerely,

L. M. Montgomery.

*On January 3, 1907, Mr. Weber thanked her for sending him a
Christmas booklet of Cavendish poetry. "I can't imagine a gift containing
more of the giver." He rejoiced with her over her hundred-dollar story.
He was still restless and yearning to write. "On Feb. 1st I shall quit
the elevator and resume practice in writing. It is so hard to find work
that will leave leisure that I may change my circumstances altogether. I
can't dismiss the ambition to write." She wrote back on February 3rd,
but her letter has not been preserved in the Weber collection. It took five
weeks to reach Mr. Weber, while the post office was making futile efforts
to guess at the address. Her hieroglyphics for "Didsbury" were suc-
cessively surmised to mean High River, Highburg, Hicksburg and Brant!
In this letter she must have reported 1906 freelance earnings as $800.
He expresses amazement at this and offers best wishes for $900 in 1907.
She was reading Gibbon again. He was busy searching for land to buy,
and he had started reading the Bible through, being "just through the
Pentateuch." He ended his letter, "the joys of Easter to you—non-
resurrectionists though we are," and signed it, "Ever fraternally and
cordially."*

Cavendish, P.E.I.,
Thursday,
May 2, 1907.

My dear Mr. W.:—

We are just in the middle of housecleaning! I fear that statement will be more or less wasted on a mere *man*. If it were made to a woman she would appreciate the compliment of my sitting down to write her after a day of it. For the past four days I've been scrubbing and whitewashing and digging out old corners and I feel as if all the dust I've stirred up and swept out and washed off has got into my soul and settled there and will remain there forever, making it hopelessly black and grimy and unwholesome. Of course I *know* it won't but knowing is such a different thing from *believing*.

Well, I must simply tell you my *great news* right off! To pretend indifference and try to answer your letter first would be an affectation of which I shall not be guilty. I am blatantly pleased and proud and happy and I shan't make any pretence of not being so.

Well, last fall and winter I went to work and wrote a *book*. I didn't squeak a word to anyone about it because I feared desperately I wouldn't find a publisher for it. When I got it finished and typewritten I sent it to the L. C. Page Co. of Boston and a fortnight ago, after two months of suspense I got a letter from them accepting my book and offering to publish it on the 10-per cent royalty basis!

Don't stick up your ears now, imagining that the great Canadian novel has been written at last. Nothing of the sort. It is merely a juvenilish story, ostensibly for girls; [but] as I found the MS. rather interesting while reading it over lately I am not without hope that grown-ups may like it a little. Its title is *Anne of Green Gables* and the publishers seem to think it will succeed as they want me to go right to work on a sequel to it. I don't know whether I can do that and make it worth while however.

The Page Co. is a good company. Not one of the top-notchers, of course, such as Harpers or Macmillans: but it has published several successful books by well-known authors, including Charles G. D. Roberts and Bliss Carman.

I signed the contract today; it is a fearsomely legal looking document all red seals and "saids" and "whereases." There is only one clause in it I don't altogether like. I have to bind myself to give them the refusal of all the books I may write for the next five years. The insertion of such a clause is rather complimentary, I suppose, but I'd rather not have to agree to it. However, I've done so and the rest is on the knees of the gods. I don't suppose the book will be out before the fall.

While I'm on the "trade" subject I might as well finish with it. I've had several successes lately; formerly I would have been delighted over them but now they are quite cast in the shade by my big fish.

The Housekeeper, Minneapolis, have accepted [a] 20,000 word serial. I am to be paid the tenth of May. Don't know what I will get but they pay well for short stories. I want you to see this story but it won't be out till next year and they want my photo to publish in their prospectus! Ha-hum!

The *Home Magazine*, Indianapolis, published by the Reader Co., recently accepted a short story to be paid for on publication. This is a new place for me.

The *Blue Book*, Chicago, paid $20 for a short story. The editor also asked me to write a 12,000 word serial of mystery and adventure but I told him I couldn't. I haven't the knack of such stories so it's no use my wasting time over them.

I got my check—for $35—from *Gunters* at last. They have another of my stories in their April number and I presume I shall have a hard time to get my cash also. I don't intend to send them any more.

There, that's enough about *me* and *my doings*. Now for your letter.

I nearly had a fit over the wanderings of my last letter. Guess I'd better typewrite the address on this if the western mail clerks are so badly afflicted with myopia.

You ask if I am ever troubled with friends I like not liking each other. Yes and yes *and* yes! I should think I know all about it. It is terrible, isn't it? Sometimes my spirit fairly cringes within me at the horror of it. I have two friends in especial whom I love and who hate each other and we are all three constantly being thrown together and my friendship with each is more or less spoiled and embittered by their antagonism.

Have you heard from Miss C. lately? I had a letter from her saying she was ill and answered at once. This was some time ago and I have not had a line from her since so I fear she is no better and perhaps worse. I am so sorry for I liked her personality very much. If I were sure her address was still the same I would write again but I do not know if it is. I suppose you never hear from Mrs. Watrous [Miriam Zieber]? Or do you?

Yes, I've read Trench's *Study of Words*—studied it at college in fact. I liked the book tremendously—although as you say I was amused at some of his orthodox biases. Words and languages are the most fascinating things in the world. It's marvellous how a language grows and develops along natural and unvarying lines. The development of its grammatical structure seems like a miracle to me. I read the other day in a magazine whose assertions carry weight that some of the most degraded and savage tribes possess languages which have a complicated and involved syntax. *How* did they get it? Well, I suppose it *grew* just as grew their bodily structure which is likewise as wonderful as that of more civilized peoples.

I congratulate you on discovering the—Bible! I did it a year ago, though and have been reading it—really, *reading* it—ever since; but as my rate of progression is slower than yours you will soon outstrip me. I can't get over much more than seven chapters a Sunday—I'm just beginning the Psalms now. It *is* a wonderful book—the crystallized wisdom and philosophy and experience of the most deeply religious people who ever existed. Could anything be more vital and truer to our own experience than this: "Hope deferred maketh the heart sick"? Could anything express a more majestic conception of God than, "Thou who inhabitest the *halls* of Eternity"?   What more beautiful than the sentence about the rainbow, "the hands of the Most High have bended it"—what more pathetic than "the heart knoweth its own bitterness and a stranger intermeddleth not with its joy"? *Job* is a magnificent thing.   Fancy the stinging irony of "Ye are the people and wisdom will die with you"!!   When I was a child a school teacher gave me a *whipping* because I used the expression "by the skin of my teeth."   He said it was slang.   If I had but known then what I know now!!!   It is in *Job*—those very words. *Ruth* is a delightful thing: "Where thou goest I will go: thy people shall be my people and thy God my God: the Lord judge between us if aught but death part thee and me."   Was ever the loving self-sacrifice and self-effacement of womanhood better or more exquisitely expressed?

I received your "buffalo" postal.   I forget whether I sent one in return.   If I did not it was because I was—and am— out of them.   I can't get any nearer than Ch'Town twenty-five miles away, so I can't always return one promptly.

Fourteen pages isn't bad for a girl who has been house-cleaning all day!   I wonder if it's absolutely necessary to houseclean?   I wonder if nine-tenths of the things we think so necessary really are so!   But I shall go on housecleaning and wondering!   I may have given up belief in fore-ordination and election and the Virgin Birth; *but* I have not and never shall be guilty of the heresy of asserting that it is not vital to existence that the house should be torn up once a year and scrubbed! Perish the thought.

Yours sincerely,

L. M. Montgomery.

While L. M. Montgomery was enjoying the heady sensation of reading a letter of acceptance from L. C. Page of Boston and of signing a pub-lisher's contract for Anne of Green Gables, *Ephraim Weber at Didsbury had taken an impulsive plunge into land speculation and large-scale farming, and was almost too engrossed even to compliment his old friend.   The prevalent land fever had finally infected him, and he had purchased 360 acres of virgin land on Dog Pound Creek about nine miles south-west of Didsbury for a cash payment and notes for \$3,500, to be* *paid off in the fall. What between shortages of barbed wire, slow delivery of fence posts, a very late spring, sick horses, "baching it" alone in a ten-by-twelve tent, brush to burn, new soil to break, wheat to seed, all the domestic and farm chores of a pioneer establishment to perform without help, he had taken on the most formidable challenge of his life.* Between April and the middle of September, he told L. M. Montgomery, he had not been able to manage a single evening at home in Didsbury free for reading and letter writing. *He was in good health, however, and his "broad acres" beside a purling stream made up "as good and beautiful a piece of land as I've ever seen."* On June 23rd he managed a respectable letter written in his tent on the prairie, full of local colour and the triumphs and tribulations of the frontiersman, and when he reached page 4 he remembered L.M.M.'s exciting news, and sent congratulations and best wishes for Anne of Green Gables, *hoping that it would go through "several editions of 10,000 each."* He is looking forward to reading her first book, he says, and discusses the comparative returns of book-length fiction and magazine stories.

L. M. Montgomery, who was also very busy with quite different matters, mailed to him from Cavendish on July 9th a picture postal card showing the beach at North Shore, and bearing the following text:

"*Letter received. This is where we go swimming. On cape at distance first recorded murder of P.E.I. was committed.*

L.M.M."

In his next letter, dated September 16th, Mr. Weber dilated on the events of his summer spent "*tenting on my bank of the Dog Pound (a beautiful stream)."* He had the "*pleasantest anticipations*" about Anne of Green Gables. *He reminds her that he is to have a fresh new photograph of her some day.* "*You see,*" he wrote, "*you must let me gather data of you, for if you die before I do, I'll write your life.* In the meantime, I'll tease you with critiques, reviews and appreciations of your work. See? The plenitude of an authoress's glory gilds her correspondents too.*" Canada needs a few more writers; he is glad she is a Canadian. "*Don't follow Roberts, Carman and Arthur Stringer to New York . . . but stay with us like 'Kit,' Drummond, Scott, Connor and Lampman.*" He ends the letter with a roll-call of his horses: "*Pat, a sorrel with silver mane, lord of the little band, Chris his mate, Doll the iron-gray with Timmy her colt—a lullabalula to look at—Nell the half broken broncho, Barny the Faithful, Teddy the chubby old timer whom I chum with, and the driving cayuses Nip and Tuck. . . . Teddy is the most intelligent looking horse I ever saw, though I have known equally intelligent ones without looking it. They are all optimists and never sour on the weather or the harness. Oh, for humans so wholesome!—of whom, thanks be, there are a number about.*"

Cavendish, P.E.I.,

Sunday Afternoon,

Nov. 10, 1907.

My dear Mr. W.:—

I did not dream when I received your letter that I should be this long in answering it—but time has slipped away so fast. October is my busiest month—full of bulb planting (delicious), housecleaning (ugh-urr-gru-u), sewing (non-excitably nice), etc., etc., etc. This rainy Sunday afternoon I am going to write some letters.

Though raining now it was fine this forenoon—oh! so fine— sunny and mild as a day in June. I hied me away to the woods— away back into sun-washed alleys carpeted with fallen gold and glades where the moss is green and vivid yet. The woods are *getting ready* to sleep—they are not *yet* asleep but they are disrobing and are having all sorts of little bed-time conferences and whisperings and good-nights. I can more nearly expect to come face to face with a dryad at this time of the year than any other. They are lurking behind every tree trunk—a dozen times I wheeled sharply around convinced that if I could only turn quick enough I should catch one peeping after me. Oh, keep your great vast prairies where never a wood-nymph could hide. I am content with my bosky lanes and the purple peopled shadows under my firs.

Three evenings ago I went to the shore. We had a wild storm of wind and rain the day before but this evening was clear, cold, with an air of marvellous purity. The sunset was lovely beyond words. I drank its beauty in as I walked down the old shore lane and my soul was filled with a nameless exhilaration. I seemed borne on the wings of a rapturous ecstasy into the seventh heaven. I had left the world and the cares of the world so far behind me that they seemed like a forgotten dream.

The shore was clean-washed after the storm and not a wind stirred but there was a silver surf on, dashing on the sands in a splendid white turmoil. Oh, the glory of that far gaze across the tossing waters, which were the only restless thing in all that vast stillness and peace. It was a moment worth living through weeks of storm and stress for.

There is a great *solitude* about such a shore. The *woods* are never solitary—they are full of whispering, beckoning friendly life. But the sea is a mighty soul forever moaning of some great unshareable sorrow that shuts it up into itself for all eternity. You can never pierce into its great mystery—you can only wander, awed and spellbound on the outer fringe of it. The woods call to you with a hundred voices but the sea has only one— a mighty voice that drowns your soul in its majestic music. The woods are human but the sea is of the company of the archangels.

I thought of Emerson's lines as I stood there that wonderful night.

> The gods talk in the breath of the wold
> They talk in the shaken pine
> And they fill the long reach of the old seashore
> With a dialogue divine.
> And the poet who overhears
> Some random word they say
> Is the fated man of men
> Whom the ages must obey.

I shall never hear that random word—my ear is not attuned to its lofty thunder. But I can always *listen* and haply by times I shall catch the faint far-off echo of it and even that will flood my soul with its supernal joy.

You spoke of death in your letter. When I said my friend had had a hard time I did not mean the actual dying—which came to her suddenly and easily—but the long weeks of horrible suffering preceding it. *That* is the real tragedy of death. I, too, hope that death will come to me *suddenly*. I don't want to *know* it is coming. I envy those who die in their sleep. You speak of chloroform. I *love* taking ether—have taken it several times for having teeth extracted. I love the sensation of going under its influence and when I come out of it I never feel one unpleasant after effect. My dentist tells me he never knew anybody like me in this respect. Just at the moment when I return to consciousness I have a fleeting *sensation* of having had the most beautiful time somewhere. Did I ever tell you of my last experience in this line? If I did pardon the repetition and skip it.

Just as I was "coming out" I heard myself saying—I put it this way because it was not *I* who said it—at least not the consciousness that is dictating these words. *This* consciousness heard *something* else speaking through my lips:

"Oh doctor, heaven is so interesting I'm sorry you called me back. I could write—a—a—a—"

I heard myself halt for a suitable word. I heard the dentist laughingly suggest "a book?"

"A book!" I heard myself scornfully casting this aside. "I could write a *lifetime* on the experiences I've been having."

And with this *I* came into my own, wide-awake and conscious, with no recollection of any such "experiences."

Wasn't it odd? I've often thought about it. It did more than anything I ever heard or read to convince me of the separate existence of the soul. And yet it raised other difficulties. For that soul was *not* I—not, as aforesaid, the consciousness that is writing to you now. But all this is more or less awkward to define. Such things can't be expressed in the symbols of earth—no words have been invented suitable for the conveyance of just exactly what I felt and how I felt it in that experience. Quite likely you will receive a wrong or at the best an utterly inadequate conception of it.

Ah, I agree with all you say of "soul moods"—states that can't be expressed or communicated because words are too clumsy!

So "if I die before you do, you'll write my life"? No, you won't! Nobody shall. I'd haunt you if you did. Biography is a *screaming farce*. No man or woman was *ever* truly depicted. Biographies, even the best, are one—or at the most two-sided—and every human being has half a dozen different sides. It must always be that way until some medium of communication is found for "soul moods." And I know I wouldn't want some of *my* soul moods depicted—no, nor any of them—for the evil ones would shame me and the good ones would be desecrated by revelation.

I am pegging away at my new book. Can't say definitely when my first one will be out. There is some hitch at present with the illustrating—artist sick or overworked or something of the sort. My "sequel" is moving on fairly well. I have everything *blocked out*—the complete skeleton, down to the last chapter. All the characters are living in my mind, all the incidents have happened, all the "talk" has been talked. I have only to write about them now.

I'm not doing much hack work. Sold a S.S. serial of seven chapters to the Toronto *East and West*. Got $40 only. It was far too cheap but Miss Fraser had been pestering me so long for a serial that I sent her one for patriotism's sweet sake. If my book succeeds I'll certainly cut out Sunday School stuff, though of course I'll keep on with adult magazines.

I'm going to tell you something. I hope it won't prove too much of a shock! The *Canadian Magazine pays* for *poetry* now. I sent it an old poem to get rid of it—the poem. It had been peddled to every American magazine and I gave it up in despair. The C.M. sent me two whole dollars for it—and asked for more! Certainly, Canada *is* forging ahead.

The *Westminster*, Toronto, also pays small sums for prose. I got $3 for a sketch. Your western sketches ought to take with them.

I enclose a *Youth's Companion* poem. Do you know I haven't written a single line of verse since July. I'm going to try to write a poem tomorrow though.

Do you know I was nearly run over by an *automobile* last night! Automobiles in Cavendish! There is no such thing as solitude left on earth!

Glad you told me about your horses. I'm sure you must love them. I only have a cat—"Daffy." But he's a *peach*! Really, he's everything a cat should be, except that he hasn't one spark of affection in his soul. But then somebody has said, "The highest joy a human being can experience is *to love disinterestedly*." *Daffy*, therefore, gives this joy to me, since I cannot hope for any return of the affection I bestow on him. The only things *he* loves are his stomach and a certain cushion in a sunny corner. He is enormous in size, with a very fine coat of grey striped fur, black points and a magnificent plumy tail. He is a mighty hunter and catches and devours *squirrels* every day. As I love squirrels also I am torn between two affections.

Well, it is nearly dark and time I was getting ready for church, since I'm organist and must sit up on the choir platform and face the audience during the service. So I dare not slur my toilette but must appear point device. At our last choir practice we practised up "Behold, the Bridegroom Cometh" for a collection anthem. Yesterday I had to summon an extra session of the choir to learn a new piece since the "supply" who preaches for us tonight really *is* a bridegroom, having been married only last week! It would have been a good joke to let the thing go on but I thought the poor man might feel insulted and ministers are so scarce that we dare not play any tricks with our chances of getting one.

Bi-bi,   Yours fraternally,

                           L. M. Montgomery.

Ephraim Weber replied on December 19th, calling the letter his "Christmas number." He reported that he was "caught in the stringency." "How is the island standing it? I don't know whether East or West is in the vise the tighter. Things are bad enough here. Everybody is 'up agin it,' but they say Vancouver is worse, and some parts of the States are getting dizzy. For me—I am certainly in a pretty kettle of fish. The one time in all my life when I made a 'plunge' was in the spring, and of course I struck this evil-starred year. I don't know how to work out my salvation now—with fear and trembling, certainly."

"Your lovely nocturne on the sea shore was a fine thing to read about," he continued. He tried to convey his own feelings about the mountains on his western skyline. Her "mood" of the woods in October gave him fine pleasure. A little group in the Presbyterian Church at Didsbury had been studying religions. He is sending her a tract, which "expresses our views here to a hair. At least the views of some twelve or fifteen. By this you see we are really Unitarians." No, he assures her, "we are not pagans here in Didsbury. We have great hopes for the religion of Jesus; but we believe in the Fatherhood of God; therefore, by logical and mathematical necessity, in the Brotherhood of Man."

Cavendish, P.E.I.,
Monday Evening,
March 2, 1908.

My dear Mr. Weber:—

No, we are not snowed in! On the contrary, we have no snow at all. We have had very little snow at any time this winter and three weeks ago a thaw took away what little there was. Since then we have been bumping about in wagons or staying at home anathematizing the weather clerk. We have had a phenomenally mild and fine winter—not one storm and very few cold days. Last Saturday morning I started out, walked five miles, spent the day with a friend, and walked home again in the evening—not bad for the dead of winter.

I have been trying to get time to answer your letter for several weeks but never could get enough to do it all at once and I cannot bear to write a letter in sections if I can possibly help it. For the past month I have been extra busy with the somewhat tedious but after all most delightful task of reading and correcting the proofs of my book. I sent the last batch back Friday, and the book is to be out about the fifteenth. I'll send you a copy and you can flesh your maiden sword of book criticism in it, always remembering that it is a story written more especially for girls and not pretending to be of any intrinsic interest to adults.

In regard to literature I've been jogging on as usual at the same old grind—an hour in the morning at magazine work, an hour in the afternoon at the typewriter, an hour in the evening at the sequel to my book. I have the latter about half done but I can't get it to suit me as well as the first. There seems to be more of a "made to order" flavour about it and less of spontaneity.

I sold the *Youth's Companion* a poem in December, "The Exile," and got ten dollars for it. I enclose a copy. *Christian Endeavour World* sent $15 for a story. I notice the journals are raising their prices. They have risen fifty per cent these last two years. I had an article entitled "The Old South Orchard" in the January *Outing*. Soon after I received a letter from an American gentleman asking me where that orchard was "because he was determined to visit it if such a thing were possible." I wrote back and told him that I was sorry to have to state that the location of the orchard was on the estates of my *chateau en Espagne*.

Last week the *Blue Book*, Chicago, sent $20 for a short story and *Forward* sent $6 for an insignificant June poem that had been declined so often by little magazines that pay from one to two dollars for a poem that I was very nearly putting it in the stove. "The Wind Bloweth Where It Listeth"—and so do editors. To all appearances, you can't account for one any more than the other!

No, we don't feel the "stringency" here at all. We suffer some disadvantages from our detached position but we have the compensating advantages. We are sufficient unto ourselves and seldom feel the worse of financial panics—at least, not unless they extend over several years. The partial failure of the western crops has blown us good as the Gov't is buying seed grain from us at high prices. I hope you will succeed in escaping from the trouble incident on the "squeeze" and I shall be glad to hear that you have done so.

I am amused and interested in the "ower true tale" you told of the "Mr. A+Miss B., etc." entanglement. But I fear it is too complicated for my pen. Kipling would glory in such a plot. Real life puts fiction to shame in the queer situations it evolves. Things *won't* go by rule. Your story reminds me of the old nursery tale of my childhood where the pig wouldn't go, the stick wouldn't beat the pig, the fire wouldn't burn the stick, etc. But in the end it wound up happily by everything beginning to do what was wanted of it. I fear few of the "real" stories develop so satisfactorily. Generally folks go on wanting something all their life or—far greater tragedy still—get it after they have outgrown the wish for it and find nothing but the outward husk of their desire left. Have you ever read *The Story of an African Farm*"? There is a little incident in it of a child who longed for a box of beautifully coloured spools her mother had.   One day her mother gave her the box and, wild with joy, she rushed away to open it.   Alas, the spools were there—but all the beautiful coloured threads were gone.   I fear life gives us many boxes of spools.

Thank you for your tract on the sympathy of religions.   I enjoyed it much and agreed with it.   Am returning it as requested under separate wrapper.   Hope I haven't inconvenienced you by my delay.   I was keeping it to show a friend who did not come until very recently.   Sometimes I wonder whether religion has been a curse or blessing to the world.   It has much that is beautiful in it but it seems also to have caused hideous suffering.   Jesus spoke no truer word than "I have not come to send peace but a sword."   Most religions have set men at variance with each other.   Nothing is so bitter and relentless as the "theologicum odium."   There are queer contradictions in these matters.   I know an old lady who is one of the sweetest kindest creatures alive.   She would not harm a fly and I have seen her weep bitterly over the sufferings of a wounded cat. But it puts her into a simple fury to even hint that a merciful and loving God will hardly burn for all eternity the great majority of his creatures.   I cannot understand this attitude on the part of so many.   Nothing seems to enrage some people so much as any attempt to take away or mitigate their dearly beloved hell.

I've been re-reading a very fascinating book lately,—*The Law of Psychic Phenomena*.   Probably I've mentioned it before. I do wish you could read it.   If it were mine I would send it to you but it is not.   I'd love to try some of the experiments in it with some mutually interested friend.   I *have* tried one or two, such as I could try alone, and have had success too.   For example, I told a friend of mine that I meant to try to make her dream of me some night.   She was to mark it down in the morning if she did but she was not to know the night I was to make the attempt.   One night before I went to sleep I began repeating in thought "I'll make So-and-So dream of me tonight" and kept it up, thinking of nothing else until I went to sleep.

She *did* dream of me that night. It may have only been a coincidence. Let us try it. When you receive this try to make me dream of you some night and if I do I'll carefully observe the date and let you know the result. Also, I'll try to make you dream of me after I think this letter has had time to reach you. It would be better to will that the dream should be horrible as we would be more likely to remember it. It is claimed that we only remember the dreams that we dream just before awakening. An unpleasant dream would probably awake us. If we can succeed it will be very interesting as establishing the possibility of mind acting upon mind, independent of matter and in defiance of time and space. Of course it will be well to remember the difference in the time between here and Alberta. It's about two or three hours, isn't it? Midnight out there would be between two and three here. So if you command your "subjective mind" to make mine dream of you during those hours it would probably contribute to the success of the experiment. I have also been trying some little experiments in "mental healing" on myself, by impressing ideas on my "subjective mind" before going to sleep, and there is certainly something in it. The book explains it all by purely natural laws and discards all "supernatural" explanations. It explains "Christian Science" along the same lines, also all manifestations of so-called spiritualism. I have found one thing anyway beyond dispute—it is a cure for insomnia. If I keep saying a thing over to myself persistently before I go to sleep one night, the next night I can put myself *at once* to sleep again by beginning to say it. The book mentions this as self-hypnotism. I believe fully that a person's "subjective mind" has great power over that person's body and objective mind but I am not at all convinced that it can influence another person. If you can make me dream of you or vice versa it will go far to convince me. Well, good-night. Laugh at my experiments if you will. They cost nothing.

Yours sincerely,
L. M. Montgomery.

E. Weber's answer to the above was dated March 20th. The financial "stringency" was sore besetting him. He had $2,200 to pay "this month," and couldn't sell, borrow or do anything about it. "I've always been against speculating, but having seen the 'specs' coin money year after year, I was at last converted to it—and of course a year too late, and was caught in the slump." The work of many years was being undone, and he was losing his assets. He is threatened with lawsuits and a sheriff's sale, but can't do a thing. "Fancy how I like it." He apologized for the mood of his letter. "The dream proposition is interesting, but I can't experiment now, for my mind is ill at ease. I have told you only half of my troubles; I have another one fully equal to the financial one on the top of it; so I can't at present disengage my thought." He pleads for a recent picture of her, even though he won't be able to afford one of himself for a year or more. "We have exchanged some dozen folios of letters now, and real letters too in this letterless age, and I think I'm entitled to your photograph." He devotes a page to theology. A Mr. Tyner, a Baptist minister, who has recently immersed some candidates in the river by chopping out the ice, has sought to quiz him on personal salvation. Had he given his heart to Jesus? "I wanted to know what he meant by that. He said, 'Trust him for your salvation.' I answered I was trusting him considerably for my salvation. But this puzzled him . . . he quoted all the bloody passages of Scripture, about atonement and vicarious suffering and 'washed in the Blood of the Lamb.' (Can you be 'reached' by such an expression?) He invoked a benediction on me and did hope I would find Jesus. I felt like saying I didn't know he was lost! and this man carries a B.A., D.D. and years of experience. Well . . ." "Do you get to see Kipling's letters on Canada?" he asks. "He certainly tries to be deep! He's about written out. 'Every dog has his day!'"

Cavendish, P.E.I.,
Sunday morning,
April 5, 1908.

My dear Mr. W.:—

I am going to answer your letter over the heads of several others having the prior claim of previous receipt because there are some parts of it I want to discuss before they grow cold with keeping.

I am very sorry to learn that you are still "on the rocks" of trouble. But as I can do nothing save express sincere sympathy and hope that you will find a way out of your difficulties, I will simply say that I do so sympathize and hope and leave it so.

I have not tried to make you "dream" yet but shall some of these times. I *did* dream of you one night—March 14th—but as you say you did not try to make me there was nothing in that. It was a foolish dream. I was visiting at an uncle's and my aunt asked me to "go to the granary and get some wheat for the hens." I went and when I opened the door you were sitting on a keg inside. I don't know how I knew it was you but I did and I was not at all surprised to see you there. You at once began telling me that you had been all through the Boer War and were giving me an account of your South African campaign when I woke up!

Dreams are usually very unaccountable. I had such a silly one one night last week. I dreamed I was *haunted by the ghost of a hat!* Everywhere I went I was attended by a black hat floating in the air beside my head. When I tried to grasp it my hand went through it in the most approved ghostly fashion. I was not frightened only annoyed because of the comment it provoked—since the hat seemed to be visible to all!

My book hasn't come yet but I am expecting it every day now. The clipping I enclose was taken from a New York paper—a publisher's foreword, of course, so counting for nothing as far as honest criticism is concerned. Of course, I don't expect there will be much criticism of any sort, good or bad. The reviews don't often take account of such small fry as juvenile books. I wonder what Miriam would have to say about my book if she knew. I'd love, just out of sheer curiosity, to hear her frank opinion of it. She has never written me since I sent her *my* frank criticism [on what] she sent for review—but perhaps that had nothing to do with her not writing. Do you ever hear from her now? I often think of her—she was a unique character in many ways, as expressed in her letters. Well, well, you know what the old Quaker lady said, "Everybody's queer but thee and me—and thee's a little queer!"

As for photograph, well, I have none of mine on hand just now and don't know when I will have any. I can't get to town for more than a day at a time twice a year and there I'm always too tired and worried to bother with photos. But whenever

I do I'll remember you, and shall hope to have one of yours in exchange.

Yes, I only do three hours' literary work a day—two hours' writing and one typewriting. I write fast, having "thought out" plot and dialogue while I go about my household work. I think the magazines really are raising their pay. Everything has gone up so I suppose they have to fall in line too. Yesterday I got $35 for an old serial from the *Housewife*. It was five or six chapters long and was much peddled,—name, "Four Winds."

Your experience with Mr. Tyner amused me very much. I have met so many men of his type. I remember one time, when I was teaching school up west I went home to dinner one day and found a "preacher" there who evidently modelled his religion after "Pansy's" fairy tales. As I sat down at the table, his very first words to me, after the formal "How do you do?" of introduction, were "*Do you live by faith?*" Although tolerably familiar with the jargon of his type I honestly didn't know what he meant, and seeing my puzzled expression he translated "Are you a Christian?" I admit I was furious at his impertinence and bad taste. I coldly said, "I might answer that question, sir, if I were not afraid that you would thereby feel encouraged to ask me if I expected to be married soon and how much money I have in the bank—since they are certainly less sacred subjects."

I don't think the creature had brains enough to understand my snub. He answered that he would not think of asking questions upon *personal* subjects!!!

I call myself a Christian, in that I believe in Christ's teachings and do my poor best to live up to them. I am a member of the church believing that with all its mistakes and weakness it is the greatest power for good in the world and I shall always do what I can to help its cause. But oh, this hideous cant of "being washed in the blood." To me that phrase always summons up a disgusting physical picture that revolts me.

By the way, just for the sake of curiosity I read *Bob Ingersoll's* lectures recently. I expected to be horribly shocked for when I was a child it was "aut Ingersoll aut diabolus." Well, I was amazed. With the exception of his disbelief in a personal God, Christ's divinity and eternal punishment—and as you know, the last two would not be exceptions with all ministers—everything he states would be admitted openly or tacitly by any minister under 40 years of age today. He was howled down because he believed in evolution and denied that the garden of Eden was a historical fact, because he denied predestination, and stated that the God of the old testament was not a deity worthy of undiluted love and admiration and denied the verbal inspiration of the Bible. These were his principal "heresies." However, the lectures were rather blatant and vulgar and his views were stated in an offensive fashion. If they were clothed in more considerate language they might be—and are—preached from the majority of pulpits today. He minces up poor old Talmage without mercy and I was with him there for I abhor Talmage and all his works—or rather sermons, for I don't think he ever *did* anything but preach vapid sensational sermons. Grandma adores Talmage's sermons—reads them every Sunday and cries over them! Well, I don't object—but I must be excused from sharing in her enthusiasm.

I don't think Kipling is "written out." I think he is just in a transition period and that he will emerge from it with something better than he has yet done. Still, of course he may not. I don't think our writers of today have the "staying power" of the older novelists. They are more of sky-rockets than of calm planetary continuance. When a man begins "playing to the gallery" he is done for.

No, *McClure's* have never printed my story yet. Of course they paid for it at acceptance. It is probably lying forgotten in the dusty corner of some editorial safe. *Everybodys* published my story last April. I thought you'd seen it. I mailed you an old copy of it yesterday. I don't think it was worth a hundred dollars—but I didn't send the check back and ask them to make it fifty, for all that!! I understand that a lady elocutionist in New York has made quite a hit with it on the platform. This letter is a fearful scrawl. I have such bad ink that I have to write large or it will blot everything. I'm written out—like Kipling—and must close. I'm going to read the Bible now— I've got as far along as Isaiah. He is splendid, isn't he? But what calamity howlers those old prophets were. And they never did any good with their scolding.

Yours sincerely,

L. M. Montgomery.

E. Weber wrote back on May 4th. "*Thank you for your sympathy while I am on the rocks,*" *he said.* *He had been forced to sell his land for sixty per cent of its value, according to some estimates, and his ten horses for fifty per cent.* *On top of it a trusted friend for whom he had backed a note for $100 had gone "to the dogs" and he had had to "fork out the stuff." He was down to his last thousand. "I'm free and beggarly again, to go as far as my bit of salvage will take me." His thoughts were again turning to authorship. He was scribbling again for practice. He picked up her reference to Ingersoll and Talmage, whom he had once read. "I can stand Talmage even yet as long as I can stand Moody, but I don't read either. They both reach beggars whom we intellectual Pharisees will never touch. And some of our own draw sustenance from these two: your grandmother and my mother for two. What you say of your being a Christian suits my case, of course. You say you stay with the church because it is the greatest power for good. I say, One of the greatest. I told a saucy orthodoxer the other day that I believe in the divinity of Jesus, only not in his deity. He required explanation, of course." Mr. Weber then discussed the poetry of Isaiah, in one of his own most eloquent passages. "Well," he concludes, "send along your book." His next was written on July 7th, to acknowledge an autographed copy of* Anne of Green Gables. "*Congratulations on having written an interesting and a wholesome novel.*" *She has depicted her Islanders, "who are wonderfully like our inland Waterloo County-ites in Ontario. And yet I'll warrant you had to do a great deal of inventing." Her characters were so interesting that he became a bit impatient at the descriptive paragraphs. However, "your P.E.I. landscapes are perfect pictures and you have gone after unhackneyed words to describe them." He discusses Anne at some length. He thought her success at school was "a little too good for the literary good of the story; but remembering Anne's many previous mis- adventures I felt a thrill of satisfaction over her exams. I do, though, enjoy a story whose hero fails tremendously." Her style will do, he says.*

Is she taking pains with it? It doesn't "read painful." He likes the book's format.

He wrote again on the following day, having apparently received a letter from her (now presumably lost) just as he mailed his of the 7th. Evidently she was able to report good early sales. "The first edition nearly all sold?!" he exclaims. "That's fine news!" He is sure she must be soaked and sated with Anne and he doubts if she can value her sequel. He believes both books will be successful. He wishes her "a sale of half a hundred thousand and much inspiration for another work." He wonders if she would like him to call Miriam's attention to her novel. He ends the letter: "A few of us are going to go to Banff on horseback—perhaps. It's 100 miles and we'd require 10 days to go and come and see. Do you ride? It would ease your nerves and headache," and signs, "Ever your friend, Ephraim Weber."

Cavendish, P.E.I.,

Thursday Evening,

Sept. 10, 1908.

My dear Mr. Weber:—

I know my correspondents all think I'm dead. I'm not—but I'm so tired and worn out, after a summer of steady grind, that I might almost as well be, as far as real *living* is concerned. To tell the truth, I feel horribly "played out."

You see, Anne seems to have hit the public taste. She has gone through four editions in three months. As a result, the publishers have been urging me to have the second volume ready for them by October—in fact insisting upon it. I have been writing "like mad" all through the hottest summer we have ever had. I finished the book last week and am now type-writing it, which means from three to four hours' pounding every day—excessively wearisome work; I expect it will take me a month to get it done—if I last so long.

Thank you for your kind remarks on Anne. I suppose she's all right but I'm so horribly tired of her that I can't see a single merit in her or the book and can't really convince myself that people are sincere when they praise her. You did not make the criticism I expected you to make and which a couple of the reviews did make—that the ending was too conventional. It was; and if I had known I was to be asked to write a second

Anne book I wouldn't have "ended" it at all but just "stopped."
However, I didn't know and so finished it up as best I could.

There has been some spice in my life so far this summer
reading the reviews. So far I have received *sixty*, two were
harsh, one contemptuous, two mixed praise and blame and the
remaining fifty-five were kind and flattering beyond my highest
expectations. So I feel satisfied as far as that goes. I wish you
could see the reviews; but as you can't I'll copy the main points
herewith. Don't think me extremely *vain* for doing so. I know
you are interested in your fellow-writer's adventures. I enclose
the Toronto *Globe* review of which I have a spare copy and you
may keep it.

Phila. *Inquirer*. "A wholesome and stimulating book."

Montreal *Herald*. "A book which will appeal to the whole
English speaking world—one of the most attractive figures
Canadian fiction has produced."

Boston *Transcript*. "Anne is one of the most delightful girls
that has appeared for many a day. She is positively irresistible."

St. John *Globe*. "A truly delightful little girl."

Pittsburg *Chronicle*. "Those who enjoy originality, quaint-
ness, and character portrayal of a high order will make a grievous
mistake if they ignore *Anne of Green Gables!* The heroine is one
of the cleverest creations in recent fiction."

Boston *Herald*. "It could only have been written by a
woman of deep and wide sympathy with child nature. A
delightful story."

Detroit *Saturday Night*. "Here's to your good fortune, Anne.
You will brighten many a career and darken nary a one."

Montreal *Star*. "The most fascinating book of the season."

Record Herald, Chicago. "Here is a literary bouquet full of
life and naturalness and quiet humour and pathos."

Milwaukee, *Free Press*. "Anne has the elusive charm of
personality. Every word she utters partakes of it and every one
of her quaint expressive ways. She is full of flavour. A better
book for girls there could hardly be for it possesses a freshness
and vivacity very rare indeed among books for girls, or indeed
among any books for children."

N.Y. *American*. "An idyllic story, one of the most delightful books we have read for many a day."

Phila. *North American*. "One of the most delightful characters in juvenile fiction—with graceful touches of fancy and in an original and captivating vein of humour."

Brooklyn *Times*. "Anne is very funny but she is not convincing."

N.Y. *Times*. "A mawkish, tiresome impossible heroine, combining the sentimentality of an Alfred Austin with the vocabulary of a Bernard Shaw. Anne is a bore."

N.Y. *World*. "The people in this book are delightfully studied and it is a pleasure to know them."

The Outlook. "One of the best books for girls we have seen this long time, with plenty of character and originality."

Buffalo *News*. "A story after the true lover's heart—full of absorbing interest from first to last."

Boston *Budget*. "A very engaging miss. She is too precocious a youngster for real life but very diverting as a book heroine. The story is fresh and entertaining and the author is to be congratulated on her maiden effort."

Chicago *Inter-Ocean*. "The most notable thing about the book is the accurate and sympathetic observation of nature."

Well, I fancy you're tired of this—so I'll let you off. One intended criticism in an otherwise favourable review tickled me immensely. "This is a very charming story but the author has missed an opportunity in her setting. Although this is Prince Edward Island which is virgin ground for a story writer, there is *nothing in the book distinctive of the place*. The scene might as well be laid in any New England village."

The italics are mine. I suppose the critic imagines that I am some American who laid the scene of her story in P.E. Island by way of getting something new in geography but who has no real knowledge of the weird and uncanny lives led by the inhabitants thereof! Another review said, "What most impresses an American is how these people of Canada *resemble ourselves*."

What did that poor man suppose we were like down here???

Now, I'll take your letter and answer your questions just as they come. You say you warrant I had to do a "great deal of inventing." Verily, yes. And not only inventing but combining and harmonizing and shading, etc., etc., etc. You *can't* describe people *exactly* as they are. The *details* would be true, the *tout ensemble* utterly false. I have been told my characters are marvellously "true to life"—nay, Cavendish readers have got them all fitted to real Cavendish people. Yet there isn't a portrait in the book. They are all "composites."

Yes, Anne's success at school *is* too good for literary art. But the book was written for *girls* and must please them to be a *financial* success. They would insist on some such development and I can't afford—yet, at least—to defy too openly the standards of my public. Some day I shall try to write a book that satisfies me wholly. In a book for the young it wouldn't do to have the hero "fail tremendously," as you say. They couldn't understand or sympathize with that. It would take older people. I do not think I'll ever be able to write stories for mature people. My gift such as it is seems to lie along literature for the young.

Yes, I took a great deal of pains with my style. I revised and re-wrote and altered words until I nearly bewildered myself.

In regard to the illustration. I thought the *second* one the best in the book—the one where she arrives at Green Gables. In it she looks almost exactly as I imagined her looking. However, I suppose the illustrations, lacking as they are in many respects, are about as good as most of those in present day fiction. The one I resented most is the bridge scene. Although in the chapter Anne is distinctly described as having "short rings of hair" she is depicted with streaming tresses!

I don't know the number of copies in an edition. That will come in the financial settling up at the end of the year. The first one would probably be small, the others larger. The publishers write me that orders have been held up for weeks waiting for the fourth edition, so that it would probably be quite a large one.

Yes, the publishers seem to be pushing the advertising well. They turn everything to account. In July a big party of

Orangemen were going on a picnic. At the Boston North St. station, they saw a copy of *Anne of Green Gables* bound in green on a newsstand. They took, or pretended to take—they were likely half drunk—the title as a personal insult, marched across to the Page building, the band playing horrible dirges, and nearly mobbed the place. One of the editors came out and told them that although the title might be offensive "the heroine, Anne, had hair of a distinct orange hue." Thereupon they "adopted" Anne as their mascot, gave her three cheers and went on their way rejoicing.

The Page Co. published an account of this incident in a dozen different papers from Boston to California. They have also set out posters and booklets galore. I am well satisfied with my publishers as far as everything has gone so far.

I pay $5 for 100 clippings to the bureau, and have found them very satisfactory.

I don't like my new Anne book as well as the first but that may be, as you say, because I'm so soaked and sated with her. I can see no freshness or interest in it. But, I suppose if I took the greatest masterpiece in fiction and read it over, say, a hundred times, one after the other with no interval between, I wouldn't find much of either in it also. I felt the same, though not so strongly, when I finished *Anne*. But I am really convinced that it is not so good from an *artistic* standpoint, though it may prove popular and interesting enough. I had to write it too hurriedly—and the *freshness* of the *idea* was gone. It didn't *grow* as the first book did. I simply *built* it. Anne, grown-up, couldn't be made as quaint and unexpected as the child Anne. The book deals with her experiences while teaching for two years in Avonlea school. The publishers wanted this—and I'm awfully afraid if the thing takes, they'll want me to write her through college. The idea makes me sick. I feel like the magician in the Eastern story who became the slave of the "jinn" he had conjured out of a bottle. If I'm to be dragged at Anne's chariot wheels the rest of my life I'll bitterly repent having "created" her.

As for Miriam—no, don't mention my book to her—unless she asks you what I'm doing.   In which case you may tell her the simple facts.   If she ever refers to it let me know, for curiosity's sake, what she says.

I have received a lot of nice letters from people about Anne. The editor of the Montreal *Herald* wrote me such a kind and encouraging letter, as did also the *Globe* (Toronto) Editor. I've been pestered with letters from "tourists" who "want to meet me."   I've snubbed all these latter politely, because I don't want to be met.   I had a letter from a lunatic in New York yesterday.   You may remember a *very* minor character in Anne is called *Priscilla Grant*.   Well, it seems his great-great-grandmother was called Priscilla Grant and he wants me to write a book about the girl in my story and call it "Priscilla Grant."   And if I do, he'll "do all he can to push it."   (He's a book seller.)

Well, there has been a great deal of pleasure in all this! But it has its seamy side as well.   I won't say much of it as I don't want to think of it.   I'll only say this.   If you want to find out just how much *envy* and *petty spite* and *meanness* exists in people, even people who call themselves your friends, just write a successful book or do something they can't do, and you'll find out!   Sometimes I feel sick at heart.   But not all are such, thank God.   I have many true friends who rejoice at my success, such as it is.   But *most* of them are outside my clan connections.

But I'm not well.   It was no joke, what I said at the start about feeling played out.   I feel so utterly.   I'm tired—deadly tired—all the time—just as tired when I wake in the morning as when I go to bed at night—tired body, soul and spirit.   I have constant head-aches and no appetite.   It's not all due to literary work, although I suppose that helped it on.   We had a houseful of guests all summer, the weather was fearfully hot and I was very much worried in one way or another almost constantly.   When I get the book done (by the way, I can't settle on a name for it and think I'll leave it to the publishers to christen) I'm going to take a good rest and not write a word for two months.   I wish I could get away for a trip and change but that is impossible as I can't leave grandma.

I've been feeling rather worse since a shock I got three weeks ago. One very hot windy day our kitchen roof took fire. There was nobody here but grandma and myself. I dragged a ladder from the barn, hoisted it against the roof (at an ordinary time I couldn't have lifted it from the ground) went up with a pail of water and succeeded in putting the fire out. Then I collapsed and had to go to bed. My nerves have been in rags ever since and I can't hear a door slam without jumping and screaming. Nice state to be in! Well, I'm taking a "tonic" and hope it will do half it claims on the label.

I'm through. This is the most appallingly egotistical letter I ever wrote. It's all about myself and my wretched book. But if I hadn't written about that I'd have *simply nothing else* to write about except social gossip that would be Greek to you.

Perhaps some day I'll be rested and leisurely and able to "imagine" something worth writing you a letter about. Oh, that reminds me. I wish I'd never written about "kindred spirits" in my book. Every freak who has written to me about it, claims to be a "kindred spirit." I'm going to dedicate my new book to "kindred spirits." *You*, therefore, will have a share in it. But many folks will *think* they have who *haven't*.

Yours tiredly, headachely, listlessly, don't careishly—but *not* hopelessly,

L. M. Montgomery.

Mr. Weber had been working on a threshing gang when he replied on October 20th. A snow storm had interrupted operations, so he was able to write. He provided Miss Montgomery with some Alberta local colour from the harvest fields. He described his duties on the threshing outfit without enthusiasm. "I don't enjoy myself, though I'm hardened to where I can endure such things. I'm sick and aching for work of my own." He apologized for pouring out his lamentations once more. "Jesus used to say, 'My hour has not come.' But a man's hour will come and then if he isn't ready! When mine comes I'll be a magazine writer. 'Twon't be long." But before the letter was finished, doubts returned. "If I don't get at writing now, I may never. It's a pivotal point I've got to. So anything you can say to encourage or discourage will be more than usually interesting."

Cavendish, P.E.I.,
Tuesday Evening,
December 22, 1908.

Thermometer 5 below zero. A raging snowstorm to boot.
Frost on window panes. Wind wailing in chimney. A box of
white Roman hyacinths sending out alien whiffs of old summers.

· · ·

My dear Mr. Weber:—

When I received your last letter on October 29th, I said to
myself, "For once I'm going to be decent and I'll answer this
letter next week." What is more, I really meant it. Yet here
it is December 22nd. Well, I couldn't help it, that is all there
is to it. I've been so busy—and so tired. I'm still the latter.
I'd love to go to bed and stay there for a whole month, doing
nothing, seeing nothing and *thinking* nothing. I really don't
feel at all well—and yet there is nothing the matter with me.
I've simply "gone stale." If you've ever experienced the feeling
I'm sure of your sympathy. If you haven't it's quite indescrib-
able and I won't try to describe it. Instead I'll just pick up
my notebook, turn back to the entry of my last letter to you and
discuss the jottings of any possibly interesting happenings since.
I daresay the most of the letter will be about that detestable
Anne. There doesn't seem to be anything but her in my life
just now and I'm so horribly tired of her that I could wish in all
truth and candour that I'd never written her, if it were not for
just two things. One of these things is a letter I received last
month from a poor little cripple in Ohio who wrote to thank
me for writing *Anne* because she said it had taught her how to
endure her long lonely days of imprisonment by just "imagining
things." And the other is that *Anne* has gone through six
editions and that must mean a decent check when pay day comes!

Well, it was September when I last wrote. We had the
most exquisite autumn here this year. October was more
beautiful than any June I ever remember. I couldn't help
enjoying it, tired and rushed as I was. Every morning before

sitting down to my typewriter I'd take a walk over the hill and feel almost like I should feel for a little while. November was also a decent month as Novembers go, but December has been very cold. Today as aforesaid has been a big storm. We are drifted up, have had no mail, and were it not for my hyacinths I should feel inclined to stop being an optimist.

Well, I've done my duty by the weather, haven't I? Of course, one had to mention it. 'Twouldn't be lucky not to.

.   .   .

I beg leave to call your attention to a new and original thought which you have not probably heard before. It is this— "every rose has its thorn." This refers to a brief and cryptic entry in my notebook for September 12th, which entry I am not going to disclose but which I shall take as a concealed text to hang a few comments on.

I've written a successful book, which will probably bring me in some hard cash. This fact has many results. One of the results is this. An old schoolgirl chum, on whom I have always been on friendly terms, suddenly becomes cool, says spiteful things of me and my book, displays incivility and rudeness to me whenever we meet and finally withdraws herself into lofty disregard of my existence. I have not "put on airs" about my book at all. Why then should she behave so? Some people say she is jealous. I hate to think so but am forced to do so. Whatever be the cause I have lost an old friend. You will say such "friendship" is not real and is better lost. I agree with you. Nevertheless, old affections rooted in childhood are lasting things and I have felt a good deal of pain over my friend's attitude.

Again, if you have lived all your life in a little village where everybody is every whit as good and clever and successful as everybody else, and if you are foolish enough to do something which the others in the village cannot do, especially if that something brings you in a small modicum of fame and fortune a certain class of people will take it as a personal insult to themselves, will belittle you and your accomplishment in every way and will go out of their way to make sure that you are informed of their opinions. I could not begin to tell you all the petty flings of malice and spite of which I have been the target of late, even among some of my own relations.

Well, I mustn't growl about this. I tell it to you merely that you need not be afraid I ought to sacrifice something dear to the gods to avert their envy. My sunshine is not so unclouded as to be a "weather breeder."

.   .   .

I've been doing very little "free lance work" since I wrote. After I finished my book MS I took a six weeks' rest from all literary [work]. It did not do me the good I had hoped. Indeed, I think I would have been better at work. I had only more time for morbid brooding over certain worries and troubles that have been ever present in my life for the past six years. They are caused by people and circumstances over which I have no control, so I am quite helpless in regard to them and when I get run-down I take a too morbid view of them. Last week I began work again by blocking out a short serial for girls.

In September the *Youth's Companion* took a poem and sent ten dollars for it, and the *Red Book* sent $25 for a story. In October the *Pictorial Review* of New York published a short story I had sent them in June and never heard from since. It was a much peddled tale, brazen from many rejections. They sent me fifty dollars for it. It was not worth ten. It *must* have been on *Anne's* merits this tale sold. Well, I'll soon be done peddling off my old MSS. I'm almost completely sold out of them now. In future I'm going to cut out all "hack work" and write up only ideas which appeal to me. Thanks to *Anne's* success I expect to be able to afford this, even should it prove a losing venture. But I don't think it will. I believe if I write solely to please myself it will "take" better than writing to please somebody else. I wrote *Anne* that way and I believe it's the only way to appeal to a large audience. But of course a writer who is struggling up can seldom afford to do this at first. I've served a long and hard apprenticeship—how hard no one knows but myself. The world only hears of my successes. It *doesn't* hear of all my early buffets and repulses.

.   .   .

Letters! Don't mention them. I have often read of the way authors were pestered with letters but now I realize it acutely. It *has* become a pest.   At first I was delighted when once or twice a week I got a nice kind letter saying nice things of *Anne;* but now they come, four or five a day, all waiting an answer.   I'm tired of writing them—I can't attend properly to my personal correspondence because of them.   Of course they are all nice and some of them are from people I am very proud to think like my book.   I think I wrote you about Mark Twain's letter. Bliss Carman and Sir Louis Davies also wrote me very kind and flattering epistles.   No, I see by my notebook Mark Twain's letter came after I wrote you.   He wrote me that in *Anne* I had created "the dearest, and most lovable child in fiction since the immortal Alice."   Do you think I wasn't *proud* of Mark's encomium?   Oh, perhaps not!

Anne went into her sixth edition on December first.   Sir Isaac Pitman & Sons, London, has brought out an English Edition.   I had a letter from William Briggs Toronto today asking to be permitted to publish my next book.   I could not do this if I wished since I signed an agreement with Page's to give them the refusal of all my books for five years.   But even if I were free I wouldn't give the MS. to a Canadian firm.   It is much better financially to have it published in the States.

The reviews keep coming in as usual.   Success seems, as usual, to have succeeded—that is they are almost all favourable now.   Since I last wrote I have had only two unfavourable ones. One said nobody over 14 years of age would find the book of interest.   In reference to that I might quote what T. H. Leavitt, Inspector of Public Libraries for Ontario, wrote me, "It is usually a sign of dotage when an old man falls in love with a young girl; but there are exceptions, such as in my case.   I am not ashamed to say that I am the old man and *Anne of Green Gables* is the young girl."

He must be over 14!

The other review wasn't very bad—just rather contemptuous. It wound up by quoting a speech of Anne's and then said, "Further than this the present reviewer did not follow the adventures of this infant prodigy so he cannot tell of what further marvels Anne was capable."

Will you believe that "this" was just to the end of the *fifth* chapter?

But I don't think some of the favourable reviewers could have read the book very carefully either. A very flattering review started off as follows: "The scene of this charming story is laid in Victoria Island near Nova Scotia. So far away, we may doubt the existence of Victoria Island but the geographies assure us of the reality of Nova Scotia. But it does not matter whether there is a Victoria Island or not; all that matters is that this is the most delightful book, etc."

What do you make of that?

The Bookman has Anne listed as one of the six "best sellers" in ten different cities. This seems to me rather like something I've dreamed. I can't really believe it.

I finished typewriting my new book the first of November and sent it to Boston the middle of the month. Haven't heard from their readers yet but don't suppose they'll reject it exactly. It's not as good as *Anne* but not so much worse as to be turned down I think.

Typewriting it almost finished me. I'd have hired it done but I knew nobody could ever make the MS. out, with its innumerable alterations, interlineations and complex notes to be inserted in scores of places. But you don't know how wretchedly tired I was when I finished. I'll never consent to be so hurried again. "What shall it profit a woman if she gain a big royalty and lose her own soul!"—getting in place of it a horrible sort of "aching void" that doesn't care enough about anything to take the trouble of it?

I suppose your threshing experiences of which you wrote so graphically are over now. (I've dropped the notebook and taken up your letter.) It must be very hard work—but at least it seems to give you a good appetite—which is what writing stories at high pressure *doesn't*. I haven't tasted anything that tasted *good* for two months. I eat by way of disagreeable duty. However, in the morning, judging by appearances now I'll have to go out and shovel snow and that honest toil will probably make me honestly hungry. "We've all got troubles of our own." *David Harum* says "a reasonable amount of fleas is good for a dog—keeps him from brooding on being a dog." The trouble is, we all think we have an *un*reasonable amount of fleas— and who is to judge?

I'm so deathly tired I'm going to stop writing for tonight though it isn't very late yet. I'll finish tomorrow night if possible.

.　　.　　.

Wednesday, Dec. 23.

I hope *this* isn't going to last all winter—more storm and bitter frost. I *did* shovel snow as predicted—there's no one we can get to do this for us—but it's all drifted back again. No mail still—and I'm ready to tear out my hair in handfuls!

Really, this has been a hard day. I haven't felt very well and am "tireder" than ever tonight. But I shall try to finish this letter—nay, I *will* finish it, even if I just have to "stop short."

Yes, I want to see you settle down to some congenial work as soon as possible. Shake off as many of your metaphorical fleas as possible, resolve to "grin and bear" the unshakeable ones, and "hoe in." Nothing but steady, persistent labour will win in literature. "Dogged does it." Why not try your hand on some essays on prairie life—the inwardness and outwardness of it, treating the subject delicately, analytically, *intimately*, exhaustively, and try your luck with William Briggs. Ten or twelve would make a book. Write on the prairie in all its aspects—by day, by night, in winter and summer, etc., etc., etc. Make each essay about three or four thousand words long and put all the airy fancy and thought into it that you can. Call the whole book *The Northern Silence* and write a title essay on that subject. Don't be in a hurry—write just when you feel in the mood for it.

. . .

Eight O'clock.

Here it is two hours later. A Christmas caller came in bringing a *duck* and a box of candy. (Write an essay on "Christmas on the Prairie" for your book!) It's really very hard to give good advice under such circumstances. But I was about through anyhow. Really, I'm in earnest. I think you could do it all right. There are many sentences and ideas in your various letters which could be worked admirably into such a series and if you decide to try it I'll copy them out and send them to you.

I must close now, for another caller has come and I do not expect to have any more spare time till after Xmas. I am enclosing the proof of the review that appeared in *National*. You may keep it. Also, as soon as I can get an envelope to fit it I'll send you a souvenir copy of my "Island Hymn," with music.

The best wishes of the season to you,

Yours very cordially,
L. M. Montgomery.

P.S. Have you heard lately from Miriam? L.M.M.

Mr. Weber answered the above letter from Vancouver. He didn't explain why he was there, though there may have been a note or postcard in between, not retained in L.M.M.'s bundles of E.W.'s letters. His father had died suddenly since his arrival at Vancouver, he wrote. The telegram had reached him after the event; and because of snow storms in the interior of British Columbia he was unable to go back to Didsbury for the funeral. He was extremely grateful to Miss Montgomery for her suggestion about prairie sketches, and was flattered that she had kept his letters. He wouldn't let her go to the trouble of hunting through them for ideas, though, until he was ready to "pledge completion of the work." Behind his Vancouver reticences, major events were looming. He had fallen in love with a teacher in Didsbury's public school. Annie Campbell Melrose was from the Eastern Townships of Quebec. He had proposed and had been accepted, and they were planning their life together. She inspired him to go on with his formal education, so as to qualify in due course as a specialist or university instructor in languages. At Vancouver he was completing his Senior Matriculation. I believe he chose that city because his old New Hampshire friend, Joseph Goodfellow, was currently residing there and he could study languages with him.

Cavendish, P.E.I.,

Sunday Evening,

March 28, 1909.

My dear Mr. Weber:

Three weeks ago I took your letter out of the box where I keep unanswered epistles and said, "I'll write Mr. W. tonight." Yet here it is three weeks later. Somehow, I never could get sufficient time all at once and I can't write a decent letter in shreds and patches. I'm writing all this not as an apology. But merely as a statement of fact.

I can't find the entry in my notebook where I wrote you last so I'll begin at "this" end of it and work backward crab fashion till I come to it. This will probably result in a rather heterogeneous epistle but "needs must, etc."

Beginning with today then, it has really been doleful in the extreme. It has been pouring rain all day and this coming on a lot of recent March snow has made fearful slush, slump and mud. The world hereabouts is so ugly that it hurts me to look on it. One can hardly believe that in a few weeks it will be all bridling and smiling in wedding finery of pink and green. God hasten the time, say I, for I long for dry ground for woodland rambles and shore reveries.

I've just stumbled by accident on the entry I couldn't find, so will just begin where I left off last time.

The New Year opened sadly for me with the sudden and unexpected death of my favourite aunt. Aunt Mary was a sort of second mother to me—a sweet, fine, brave, plucky little woman who had lived a more truly heroic life than many of the heroes and heroines of history. She had a very dissipated husband and all the care of providing for and educating her family of six fell on her. She did it so triumphantly that every one of them is today occupying an honourable social station and a prosperous financial condition. Then, her work done and tired out, she died—"after life's fitful fever she sleeps well." If she could have but lived ten years to enjoy the ease and pleasure her children were so eager to give her!

I felt her death bitterly; but these things can't be written about!

I have not been especially well this winter. Yet I hate to complain when there is so much worse suffering everywhere. I've been very nervous and at times somewhat morbid. The doctor says my nervous system is run down and requires a course of raw eggs and cod liver oil. I find I'm improving under such regimen and this last month I've been much better, though I still get very tired far too easily and quickly.

Signed the agreement for my new book the other day, on the same terms as before. It is to be called *Anne of Avonlea*—the publishers' christening. I wanted it *The Later Adventures of Anne*. It is not to be out before next fall. They write me that *Anne* is still selling as well as ever and they do not wish to give her a rival as long as that continues.

I had *such* a funny letter from a man the other day who had read my book. He seems rather an illiterate person but his letter was passable till it came to the postscript. "I am a married man so you will understand that my motive in writing to you is only friendship." There's a thoughtful man for you! *He* is not going to arouse any vain hopes in the bosom of a poor literary spinster!

The flood of letters continues. Some of them are very nice. A great many English people have written to me. I enclose a few criticisms from English papers.

In February I got my first royalty cheque for the amount due me up to the close of the year. It was for seventeen hundred and thirty dollars. Not bad for the first six months of a new book by an unknown author, I think. I get nine cents out of the wholesale price of 90c. It seems rather disproportionate to the publisher's share; but I suppose when you consider that they've got to run their business out of the profits as well as make up for what they lose on books that don't succeed it is not likely they clear much more than the author after all.

If you can get hold of a book by Bliss Carman called *The Making of Personality* read it. I know you'll find it both delightful and helpful. I did. A friend lent it to me lately and I thought so much of it I'm going to send for it for my own library. It embodies a fine and excellent philosophy of life and has the charm of beautiful literary finish besides.

Now for your letter:—

So you have removed to Vancouver. You don't exactly say you like it, or the reverse. I've heard much in its praise but I don't fancy I'd like to live there. I have a lawyer uncle there, my mother's brother, Chester B. Macneill. So you are—or were—rooming at a Christian Scientist's. Well, I hope her "science" will guard her unlocked doors! It is laughable to see the extremes to which the human mind will go. I believe there is a good deal in mental healing, where no organic disease is present, but I fear 'twould prove a poor defence against a sneak thief were he "so dispoged." Are you following the Emmanuel Movement in Boston? I am and feel considerable interest in it. It is practically Christian Science purged of its absurdities. Last fall I was reading some of its articles and decided to try to cure myself of sick headaches, from which I had suffered every few weeks for eight years. I've been to several doctors and tried all sorts of medicines—got eyeglasses but though there was a very slight improvement it was not a cure and did not last. Well, I began last November. Every night when I found myself dropping off to sleep I would repeat to myself "Remove the cause of my headaches." I really hadn't the least faith in it. But it is a simple fact that I have never had a headache since I began! I discontinued the "treatment" after a month but there has been no return of the headaches. I am not *altogether* convinced—it is possibly only a coincidence and they might have stopped anyhow. But I am "almost persuaded" that it was the mental suggestion which did it. Anyhow "faith" had nothing to do with it, for I had none.

I have been trying to cure my nervous trouble but can't see that it did any good—although perhaps my present improvement is the result of it instead of my tonics!

Did you get the copy of my Island Hymn? I sent it to Didsbury before I knew of your change of location. I believe it was sung and presented as a stage picture at a concert in the Opera House in town the other night. The author and composer were called before the curtain and cheered. But only the composer could respond. The author couldn't go. She had to stay home and wish she could.

In regard to photos—I intend to have some new ones taken in the spring and *if* they are decent I will send you one. My pictures seldom resemble me. I am a petite person with very delicate features; my photos, at least the "head and bust" ones represent me usually as a strapping personage with quite a large pronounced face. The last one I had taken—the one that has been so generously scattered over the continent in magazines and advertisements, was considered good of me. I sat for one the other day as the Page Co. insisted on a new one for the *Book News Monthly*. They wanted a head and shoulders picture and the result is not like me, though passable as a picture. I am not having any finished from it. I shall be very much pleased to have one of yours in return any time you may be ready to send it.

You have my sympathy in regard to your father's death. I have had a double experience of those brutal telegrams announcing the death of a dear one. They are like a blow in the face. A letter softens it a little but a telegram cannot. I think a sudden death is hard on the survivors; but I agree with you fully that is the most desirable of deaths for the one most vitally concerned. I pray I may die so. I don't want to *know* I'm going to die. And yet I have a horrible fear that I'll die by inches, as you say. When I read of someone having died in his sleep I always envy him. What a strange thing this death is. We all know we are going to die sometime but the knowledge never worries us or clouds our happiness here, as a general thing. Theologians have done much to surround death with horror and dread. If we listened to Nature's teachings we should be happier, truly believing (I hold) that death is simply a falling asleep, probably with awakening to some happy and useful existence, at the worst an endless and dreamless repose. Isn't the Christian (?) doctrine of eternal torment as *hellish* as the idea it teaches? How could men ever have so libelled God? They must have judged Him from their own evil hearts. *They* would have tortured their enemies eternally if they could. God had power, therefore He would. Such seems to have been their argument. I admit that a consciousness of sin and remorse is a hell in itself. But I believe that "as long as a human soul lives it can turn to God and goodness if it so will." Nobody *wilfully* chooses evil. We choose it because we deceive ourselves into thinking it good and pleasant. When we find that it isn't we turn from it. Sometimes, in the case of bad habits, we cannot turn from it. But I believe that only lasts while the physical body on which the habit is impressed lasts. When it is destroyed the habit will also be destroyed and the liberated soul will get "another chance," with the warning of its bitter experiences.

Well, we believe and believe. Some day we'll know—or else there will be no curiosity.

I find I'm getting tired. I can't write as long at a stretch without growing weary as I could formerly. So I'll say goodnight. I'm going to address this to Didsbury as I'm not certain where you may be. They will probably forward it.

Yours faithfully,

L. M. Montgomery.

P.S. Please do not mention to anyone how much my royalty was.

Over three months elapsed before Mr. Weber wrote back, though a card came from Cavendish some time in between, reporting that L.M.M. was reading proofs of Anne of Avonlea; *and he may have sent a card in reply. He replied to the above letter on a Sunday evening, July 11th, having just come from the Methodist church service, at which he had heard a good sermon by "a Dr. Bland of Winnipeg." He had recently been an usher, in the Vancouver Opera House, for a convention of the World's Congress of Women, and he reported on some of the sessions. This inevitably led him to discuss "the Woman's question," suffrage for women, and "equal pay for equal service." He wished married women everywhere "were real companions to their husbands," and asserted that "the private and semi-public spheres are wide ranges for able women." Through hints and oblique references what he was doing in Vancouver now came out. When he wrote in July, he had just finished a week of exams, and was awaiting results from the provincial capital, Victoria. Meantime he had already enrolled in an extra-mural university course at Queen's, Kingston, Ontario. He wonders what L. M. Montgomery thinks of his decision to go teaching again? He has so little difficulty with English and languages, he says, that as soon as he can afford it, he will specialize in these subjects and work into a High School. "I could give you a few reflections on my going back to teaching after all these futile years—and so could you. Well, if I didn't have to start at the bottom again to earn my very bread, I'd keep following 'the Gleam,' but now if I ever write again 'twill be as an avocation. Possibly the gleam will be come at that way as soon as any. I can't leave off wanting it. A few things once glimpsed can nevermore be done without. It seems to me a thing of beauty is a joy and torment forever."*

A later communication (not in the Weber file) told Miss Montgomery that he was leaving Vancouver for Calgary, where he intended to enroll in the Normal School and qualify for a professional teaching certificate. Though he did not say anything about it in his letters, he could hardly discuss a date for his wedding until he had the prospect of a regular income.

Cavendish, P.E.I.,
Thursday Evening,
Sept. 2, 1909.

My dear Mr. Weber:—

I have been waiting for weeks in the vain hope of getting enough time to write you a decent letter "at one fell swoop," and not simply by fits and starts—five minutes now and ten minutes later on, as most of my letters have been written this summer. We have had a houseful of company and I've been *so* busy!

This is a good evening for letter writing, insomuch as it is pouring rain, and therefore I am not likely to be interrupted by callers. But I have a cold and headache and so am not exactly in the mood for writing. But I must not delay any longer, for I want to acknowledge your photo which came a few days ago and I was vastly pleased to get. I cannot, of course, judge if it is "true to life" but it looks as if it ought to be. Thank you very much for it. I have one to send you in return, but I shall not forward it until I am sure your present address will "stay put" long enough for you to get it, or it may go astray. When you receive this letter drop me a postal with your permanent address and I'll forward the photo "immediately and to onct." My friends like it. They say it is very like me in the face but my figure looks much too stout in it. I'm really very slight.

Well, I've been very busy all summer and yet I've accomplished *nothing*. A satisfactory epitome of a summer, is it not? Our guests left last week, however, and now I mean to settle down, if possible, to a good autumn's work. I've begun work at a new book, with a new heroine. It's to be called *The Story Girl* and I have the *first sentence* and the last paragraph written!

The new Anne book is out—I got my copies day before yesterday. We soon get used to things. I was quite wild with excitement last year on the day my first book came. But I took this one very coolly and it caused merely a momentary ripple on the day's surface. Its "get-up" is very similar to the first. You're to get a copy. I ordered it sent to you direct from the publishers to "Calgary, Alberta," so be on the look-out for it if you move on. I enclose an autograph card which you can paste on [the] fly-leaf if you wish.

I am glad they did not illustrate this book, except for the frontispiece. I did not like the illustrations in the first one. The painting of Anne Shirley will do. It isn't "my" Anne, but doesn't glaringly violate what she might be.

Now for your letter:—

So you attended a meeting of the World's Congress of Women! Do you know, I was actually asked to read a paper before that august assemblage in Toronto. I had no difficulty in refusing to do that; but I should have liked to attend the congress, if I could have got away. It would be a very broadening experience, I fancy.

As for the woman suffrage question, I feel very little interest in it. But I *do* believe that a woman with property of her own should have a voice in making the laws. Am I not as intelligent and capable of voting for my country's good as the Frenchman who chops my wood for me, and who may be able to tell his right hand from his left, but cannot read or write?

So you wish "married women everywhere were real companions to their husbands." So do I—as heartily as I wish that married men everywhere were real companions for their wives. You can't, as Emerson says, cut this matter off with only one side. It has to have two. As for "spheres," I believe anyone's sphere—whether man or woman—is where they can be happiest and do the best work. The majority of women are happiest and best placed at home, just as the majority of men are in the world. But there are exceptions to *both*. Some women are born for a public career, just as some men are *born to cook in a restaurant*. Yes, they are! And each has a right to fulfil the purpose of their birth. Sex seems to me to enter very little into the question. There is no sex in mind, I do believe, and—"let each one find his own," and her own, in business as well as matrimony.

Have you heard from Miriam lately? Does she ever mention me? Does she know about my books? Poor Miriam, I was reading over some of her hectic epistles the other day and enjoyed them as curious character studies. What sort of a husband has she got if he can't keep her decently.

Yes, I advise you to specialize on English and languages as soon as you can. This is the age of specialization and I believe you could do excellent work along that line (I see the *Bookman* has tabooed the expression "along that line"—consigned it to its "inferno," but it's too too convenient to give up, and would probably enjoy teaching it. I do not think you need give up "following the gleam" because you are going back to teaching again. Thank God, we can always follow the gleam, no matter what we do. I've tried to follow it for many a weary year—*how weary*, no one knows but myself, for I've always tried to keep my personal worries and crosses to myself, not allowing their bitterness to overflow into others' lives.   But I've reached a bit of upland now and, looking back over the ascent, some things are made clear to me that have long puzzled me.   But there's lots of climbing to do yet.   I must take a long breath and start anew. If I can only write my new book up to my conception of it, it will be away ahead of *Anne* from a literary point of view.   But I know I shan't be able to—

> Did ever on painter's canvas live
> The power of his fancy's dream?

Still, I'll do my best and it will surely be a step in advance. Do you likewise take heart of grace and "follow knowledge like a sinking star" to the utmost bound of your endeavour.   You know what Keats says—

> He ne'er is crowned
> With immortality who fears to follow
> Where airy voices lead.

Follow your "airy voices" fearlessly and they'll lead you to the heights.

The only thing I've written since May is a series of four articles on the words in the four seasons.   I put a good deal of blood into them but don't know whether they're worth while after all.   I don't know either just what magazine they'll do for. I enjoyed writing them so perhaps people will enjoy reading them.   It's a fairly good test.

I've done a lot of "gadding" this summer, and it was really a horrible waste of time because there was no pleasure in it. Had there been, I'd have considered it a very wise use of time. I had to go out to tea and attend garden parties galore and I was generally bored to death, especially when people thought themselves bound to say something about my book.   They all say practically the same thing and I say the same thing in reply and I'm tired of it.   Then I talked gossip and made poor jokes and altogether wished I were home in my den with a book or a pen.   Not that I don't enjoy *real* conversation.   There is nothing

I enjoy more. But it's not once in a thousand times I get it and anything else is like brown sugar in the god's nectar. "For every idle word ye speak ye shall give account in the day of judgment." May the Lord have mercy on my soul! I have talked idle words by the *million* this summer.

By the way, what a vital thought that is—like so many other thoughts in that wonderful old Bible. "*Idle* words." Not bad words, or bitter words, or wicked words! They have some strength and purpose and vitality in them that *almost* justifies them. But *idle* words,—words that desecrate the sacredness of language meant to convey heart and soul's deepest meaning to heart and soul, debased coin of speech that discredits the image and superscription of the godhead inscribed on it; weak words, silly words, *empty* words, "sounding brass and tinkling cymbals"— yea, verily, 'tis of these we must give account, and who of us have not so sinned?

By the way, I had a good laugh today over a card that came to me addressed to "Miss Anne Shirley, care of Miss Marilla Cuthbert, Avonlea, Prince Edward Island, Canada, *Ontario.*" In the correspondence space was written "Dear Anne, I am sending you a picture of the floral clock in our park at Detroit, Michigan, from a friend." No name was signed to it. The writing was very unformed so I presume it is from some kiddy who fondly imagines that all the people in books live "really and truly" somewhere. A p.o. clerk in town had written across it, "Try Miss Montgomery, Cavendish," so it reached me.

I think it was since I wrote you that I received a copy of the London *Spectator* reviewing Anne. It honoured me with a two column review and was exceedingly kind and flattering. I *did* feel flattered. The *Spectator* is supposed to be "the" review of England and praise or blame from it makes or mars. It wound up by solemnly warning me *not* to make a sequel so when it sees I've disregarded its advice I expect it will justify my warning by "slating" my new book. But I'd rather be *abused* by the *Spectator* than ignored,—or even *praised* by many inferior sheets. I can't really believe that my little yarn, written with an eye single to Sunday School scholars, should really have been taken notice of by the *Spectator*.

What are you doing in Calgary? Teaching? A cousin of mine, Laura McIntyre, has just gone to Calgary as a bride—Mrs. Ralph Aylesworth. If you come across her tell her to be good to you for my sake!

This new sheet is simply to say good-bye on. Write when the spirit moves. I'm always glad to hear from you, even if I am slow in answering. That isn't my fault but my misfortune.

Yours faithfully,
L. M. Montgomery.

Epilogue

VIII

L. M. Montgomery's letter of September 2, 1909, is the last of the extant "Cavendish" letters to Ephraim Weber. Several more were written between then and the time of L. M. Montgomery's marriage in 1911, as we know from his side of the correspondence, but they have been lost. Drastic changes in his life were imminent, and his part in the correspondence faltered for a time. In the spring of 1911, L. M. Montgomery's aged grandmother died, setting her free at last to leave the old home. A visit to Boston followed. In July of that year she was married at Park Corner, P.E.I., to the Rev. Ewan Macdonald. They left Canada at once on a long honeymoon trip in England and Scotland. In September the Macdonalds took up residence in Ontario. The correspondence with Ephraim Weber, which had never entirely ceased, was now actively resumed. The character of it inevitably changed, of course, and so did the frequency: it tended to take the form of longer and longer "annuals." L. M. Montgomery's later letters illustrate her growing intellectual and descriptive powers. To the very end she was a shrewd critic of men, manners, books, and affairs. They form a valuable commentary on segments of Canadian life between 1916 and 1939. But the earlier "Cavendish" letters, with their fresh lyrical charm, constitute a unit in themselves, and as such have been presented here.

In a sense my task as editor is complete with the printing of her letter of September 2, 1909. But readers might feel that I had unpardonably left them up "in the air" if I failed to add a few paragraphs about the later fortunes of the man whose personality helped to inspire such fascinating letters. The main events of L. M. Montgomery's career are public knowledge. But what happened later to Ephraim Weber? Did they ever meet? And did he ever make good his "threat" to write her biography?

When the September, 1909, letter reached him, Ephraim Weber was embarking on a radical new course in life. In the next seven years the erstwhile broncho-buster, farm speculator, freelance bachelor of homestead tent and "den," undertook to become a learned grammarian and a university don. He enrolled at Calgary Normal School about the time L. M. Montgomery was penning her September, 1909, letter. He graduated just before Christmas, with a certificate authorizing him to teach in Alberta schools. On Christmas Day he was married, at Calgary, to Miss Annie Campbell Melrose, the Didsbury school teacher who had encouraged him to make one more determined effort to realize his scholastic dreams. After a short honeymoon, they took up residence in Calgary, where he found a post as vice-principal of Haultain Public School.

His marriage was singularly happy, but the path toward his academic and literary ambitions continued to be thorny. His eyesight was taxed throughout his Normal School course, and he found teaching no more congenial than he had fifteen years earlier. By the end of the first school term (June, 1910) he was close to a nervous breakdown. A summer at Didsbury, in the fields, restored his health; but he and his wife decided to give up school for a year. They set out for Kingston in the fall so that he could register at Queen's University in German, French and English courses, looking toward the degree of Master of Arts in Modern Languages.

To help finance his university education both of them counted on teaching "summer" schools. And their life settled down into that pattern,—a fall and winter term at university, then a summer on the prairies, teaching school. Once or twice while he was at university Mrs. Weber stayed in the West and taught school right around the calendar.

In this way he completed in three years the requirements at Queen's for the M.A. He won the university gold medal in both German and French. For a year he was a tutor at Queen's in German, in charge of German dramatics. Then in 1914 the Webers moved to the University of Chicago. By now he was aiming at the Ph.D. and a post in German language and literature in some university. He chose for his thesis topic, *The English Translations of Faust*. In the fall of 1916 it seemed highly probable that the dreams he and Miss Melrose had woven together at Didsbury would come substantially true.

At this point, however, he suffered a major setback. The entry of the United States into the war in 1917 killed all hopes of a university teaching post. German departments were being rapidly closed up all over the country. It became impossible for him to obtain from Europe some of the works on Goethe he needed for his thesis. To cap it all, after months of toil on his thesis topic, he found that an earlier scholar had covered much of the same ground. He had been within sight of obtaining his doctorate, since he had completed all the required classwork; but now he sensed the futility of it all, and eventually allowed his credits at the University of Chicago to lapse. The doctorate had eluded him.

The summer of 1917 found him, in consequence, at loose ends, with a great deal of university education behind him, but otherwise in much the same economic position as at Calgary seven years earlier. As before, he could choose to make a living by farming or teaching school. The Webers returned to western Canada late in the summer of 1917, and he picked up the first available school he saw advertised in the *Manitoba Free Press*. He became teacher of the senior room of a two-roomed village school at Lajord, Saskatchewan, about twenty-five miles southeast of Regina. Lajord, he wrote to Mrs. Macdonald (now mistress of the Manse at Leaskdale, Ontario), was "a scrubby, mangey, mildewed residue of retrogression" with a cosmopolitan mob of Canadians, Americans, Scandinavians, Germans and French-Canadians. The intellectual life of the community was "somewhat above that of the Valley of Jehosophat." However, there were "several semi-kindred spirits in it."

IX

His references to Lajord were of particular interest to me, when I encountered them in his correspondence, because it was at Lajord, in early June of 1918, that I first met Ephraim Weber, with consequences of great moment for my own future life. I was in Lajord as a junior clerk in the Standard Bank of Canada, having been recently transferred there from my father's old homestead country fifty miles south of Medicine Hat.

As this book, too, ultimately owes its existence, through a long chain of circumstance and coincidence, to that June, 1918, meeting between us, I may be pardoned for recalling one or two personal details. I attended the Presbyterian Church at Lajord on the first Sunday I was there. Mrs. Weber, I remember, played the organ, and Mr. Weber sang in the congregation, which numbered about a dozen. The Webers took due note of the presence of a stranger, a lonesome-looking seventeen-year-old, I have no doubt, and invited me to come and take Sunday lunch with them. He must have been the first scholar and "literary" person ever to invite me to his home: I was profoundly impressed by his library of college texts and classics, his L. C. Smith typewriter, and all the paraphernalia of the freelance. I recall that we talked about universal languages, such as esperanto; I believe that he read me a few paragraphs in that language; but nothing more comes back to me now. In any event the ice was hardly broken in that first meeting. What drew us together was a more lively exchange in the village store one Saturday night a few weeks later. This began on an odd note. I had been helping the storekeeper to handle his heavy Saturday evening traffic, which had now subsided, and I was sitting on the counter kicking my heels when Mr. Weber came along and made conversation.

"What do bank clerks do with their spare time?"

"I read," I said.

"Detective stories?"

"No," I said quite honestly, but a bit smugly, "I'm working my way through *Paradise Lost*!"

That led to more serious conversations, and before the winter was over we were spending much time in each other's company. He encouraged me to leave the bank and attend Regina Collegiate. (There had been no High School at all in the Manyberries country where I was brought up.) In June of 1919, I met the Saskatchewan Junior Matriculation requirements. On the strength of that I obtained a permit to teach rural school in southern Alberta. Then I went to live with the Webers for six months at Outlook, Saskatchewan, where I successfully prepared myself for the Senior Matriculation exams in 1920. The door to further education then lay wide open to me and I took advantage of it. I have little doubt that if I had not met Ephraim Weber on that June Sunday on the Regina Plains my formal schooling would never have gone beyond that of the one-roomed rural school of the old homestead days.

X

Mr. Weber was in his forty-seventh year when he left the University of Chicago. He taught steadily thereafter until he was sixty-three, always in Saskatchewan schools: Lajord, Outlook, Oxbow, Battleford. Teaching still went against the grain, for the most part, but he was endlessly conscientious about it, and with many of his students he was highly successful. One inspector in 1930 called him "the best teacher of literature in

Saskatchewan." This did not save him from being let out by the Battleford Collegiate Board in 1933, at the depth of the great depression. He could soon have found another post, in all probability, but by then he had had enough. The Webers decided to retire on their modest savings and give him a belated chance to write. The first project he tackled was an essay on "L. M. Montgomery as a Letter Writer."

L. M. Montgomery and Ephraim Weber met "in the flesh" three times. In July, 1928, the Webers visited the Manse at Norval in the course of an automobile tour through Eastern Canada. The second time it was Mrs. Macdonald who was on tour, in October of 1930. The third and last time was in the summer of 1935, when the Webers were again touring in the East and saw L. M. Montgomery in Toronto.

Neither side of the Montgomery-Weber correspondence yields much detail about these face-to-face meetings, but after their October meeting of 1930 at Battleford (he was teaching English and Latin at the Collegiate there) he provided me (at the Press Gallery in Ottawa) with some impressions of her visit:

"In mid-October, during that blizzard we had for guest twice overnight, L. M. Montgomery. I went for her to N. Battleford in the mail-carrier's big rough sleigh, carrying a blanket and Mrs. W's winter coat for our guest. No taxis ventured out that night. It was no princely ride she got in that chaotic sleigh as it screeched over the gravel and over those long bridges. But her sportly temperament enabled her to see the gruff humour of the West in it. She consented to have the Collegiate call a meeting and she read passages from her works, prose and poetry. She reads well and has an impressive presence on the stage, though she is short. The girl students were enraptured with her, especially those who had read her Anne and Emily books. She had to autograph a few dozen volumes. She met some of her enthusiastic readers at our house after the meeting, and was amused at the dissatisfaction of one of them, who thought that Emily should have married Teddy instead of Dean, even insisting on it after hearing the author's explanation. I read to the crowd at our house a most original and a most hearty appreciation of a scene from *Magic for Marigold*. The author seems to be hardened both to praise and blame, though she can still appreciate appreciation. She told the collegiate audience that she and I have exchanged literary and general epistles for thirty years; and that I and one English friend were the only two who persisted in making a correspondence worth while throughout three decades. It was an honour to have a world-famous author as guest. Her initial book, *Anne of Green Gables*, has been translated into French, Dutch, Swedish, and Finnish, and has seen well over a million copies of itself. She is so modest that one has to ask to learn much."

The correspondence which had begun in 1902 ended without much warning nearly four decades later. The last letter she wrote Ephraim Weber contained no premonitory signals. She had been indisposed but felt like new again, she said. Her letter ran to twenty-seven pages, and was the usual delightful *mélange* of poetry and penetrating comment on the ways of the world. She was still writing lyrics, and quoted the latest one for him. Mr. Weber took his time in acknowledging her letter, but when he did so he wrote back confidently that he and Mrs. Weber were "looking forward to her annual epistle." But no more annual epistles came then or ever after. The correspondence was essentially over. There were three more brief notes, little more than medical bulletins from her bedside, and then the newspaper item recording her death in April, 1942. Some time before her death she knew that she would never recover, and faced the fact bravely. "Let us thank God," she said in one of these final notes, "for a long and true friendship."

XI

In the early summer of 1933 he had forwarded to her his 4000-word sketch on "L. M. Montgomery as a Letter Writer," in which he had quoted from some of the letters in this collection. She enjoyed reading the essay, and told him that "it had an odd resurrective power and made the dead Past live again. Some of the phrases I had completely forgotten and they came to me as if someone else had written them. There is nothing I object to, so as far as I am concerned, go ahead and publish." She suggested several possible markets. Mr. Weber tried all of these in turn, but the article was not accepted.

After L. M. Montgomery's death, he revised the article and submitted it to *The Dalhousie Review*, where it finally appeared in the issue of October, 1942. Encouraged by its publication, he then wrote a study of the character "Anne" as she appeared in the eight "Anne" novels. This also was published, in the April, 1944, issue of *The Dalhousie Review*. Several similar studies were in manuscript among his papers at the time of his

death, but I believe that the two articles cited above were the
only biographical and critical studies of her ever to appear under
his name.

   The publication of his first article in *The Dalhousie Review*
led to a suggestion by "some friends" that he should write her
biography. (I find this item among his letters.) The idea
vaguely attracted him, but he was sceptical about his powers at
his advanced age, and wondered whether he could count on the
necessary co-operation of friends and relatives of the late novelist.
So far as I know the project went no further.

   Ephraim Weber outlived L. M. Montgomery by fourteen
years. He was granted a long and tranquil evening of life, and
when he died it was in the gentle sudden manner both of them
had felt, in their 1909 exchange on this solemn theme, was such
a desirable boon. One morning in March, 1956, he was
working with his papers on the kitchen table at Victoria, when
he laid his head down among them and went to sleep. His wife,
nearby, occupied in preparations for lunch, noted the slump of
his head forward on the table, but by the time she reached him it
was all over.

XII

   When L. M. Montgomery was buried in the graveyard at
Cavendish, not far from the plot in which her youthful mother
had been laid, the funeral address was delivered by the Rev. Dr.
Frank Baird, representing the Moderator of the Presbyterian
Church. The tribute appeared shortly afterwards in *The
Presbyterian Record*, and gave rise to some correspondence between
Dr. Baird and Mr. Weber. Both of them were intense admirers
of L. M. Montgomery's literary gifts, and they vied with one
another in finding phrases to express what they felt. Both of
them were reminded of George Eliot's famous prayer:

> O may I join the choir invisible
> Of those immortal dead who live again
> In minds made better by their presence.

   This theme, the immortality of personal influence, was often
in Ephraim Weber's mind; and in a letter to Dr. Baird he went
on to quote, as he had quoted more than once to me in the past,
a haunting quatrain he had encountered half a century before

in a Sunday School magazine.   It was John B. Tabb's comment upon personal influence:

> He cannot, as he came, depart,
> The wind that woos the rose:
> Her fragrance whispers in his heart
> Wherever hence he goes.

This quatrain Dr. Baird had not seen before, and he found "material for a whole sermon" in Ephraim Weber's further words on the influence of his poetic correspondent of the long ago:

"This exalted rose-function—who in these hard latter decades has performed it better to all the world's dreary winds that seek solace than L. M. Montgomery?"